DON'T FALL FOR YOUR BROTHER'S BEST FRIEND

LOGAN CHANCE

Copyright © 2024 by Logan Chance

All rights reserved.

No part of this book may be reproduced in any form or by any electronic or mechanical means, including information storage and retrieval systems, without written permission from the author, except for the use of brief quotations in a book review.

No part of this book was written with Artificial Intelligence. I support human creativity, and will never use generative AI.

Cover Design by: Kate Farlow with Y'all That Graphic

For all of you who pick up this book, thank you for giving me a chance.

Special Gift

WANT MORE SEXY ROMANTIC READS?
Sign up for my mailing list and receive a FREE copy
of my novella RENDEZVOUS.
CLICK HERE to claim your book.

Prologue

Griffin
Four Years Earlier

Sunday dinner with the Atwood family is a lifelong tradition, a ritual that holds a special place in my heart. It's been a while since I was here, but after finishing culinary school, I'm back in Magnolia Ridge. It feels good to be home. It feels great to be with my best friend, Callum, again. He's the brother I never had, the only person who knows my secrets. Without him and the Atwood family, I'd have no one.

Now that I've earned my culinary degree and Callum has finished his training to become a brewmaster, we can finally build our dream—a brewery.

While Carol, Callum's mom, is busy in the kitchen, and Don, his father, is outside with Tripp and Brock, Callum's youngest brothers, I'm sitting with Callum, Shepherd, and Paxton at the dining room table. Callum is the oldest, followed by Shepherd, who's more of a lone wolf. He enjoys staying home and working around his house. Next is Paxton. He's probably the most rambunctious of the group. He loves beer, and I think the brewery may have even been his idea when we were in high school. After Paxton is Anya, and what can I say about Anya? She's tough. You'd kind of have to be, to be the only girl with an onslaught of guys in the house. After her is Brock. He's strong, and confident, and loves the outdoors. Lastly is Tripp, the baby of the family. He's your typical kid. Loves video games and that's about it.

The aroma of Carol's cooking wafts through the house, a comforting mix of spices and roasted meats that brings back countless memories. Laughter and the sounds of clinking glasses fill the room as the family catches up on the week's events. It's a lively, bustling atmosphere that I've missed dearly.

"So, how does it feel to be back?" Shepherd asks, leaning back in his chair and regarding me with a smile.

"It feels incredible," I reply. "I've missed this—the noise, the chaos, and especially Carol's cooking."

Paxton grins. "Yeah, Mom's food is something else. You're in for a treat tonight. She's making her famous lasagna."

Callum nudges me. "And don't forget, we've got our brewery plans to discuss. We've been dreaming about this for years, and now it's finally happening."

I nod, excitement bubbling up inside me. "I know. I can't wait to get started. We're going to make something amazing."

The four of us continue talking about getting the brewery going and I can't remember a time I've been more excited about something. Callum will own the brewery outright, and bring me on as the head chef. I wish I had the money to buy-in, but that's just not in the cards right now. Maybe someday I can.

We're young, Callum and I are the oldest at twenty-three, while Shepherd is twenty-two, and Paxton is twenty-one, but we're ready. We're all in. This idea is something we've had for years and I know it's going to be a success.

"So, the old power plant is for sale and I think it's the perfect location. The building is huge, the property is great, and there's so much we can do with it. Dad and I already talked to his realtor friend who has it on the market and he's willing to cut his commission in half," Callum says, crossing his arms as he looks between us.

"That sounds amazing," I say.

"Yeah, I think we should all go for a tour and check it out," Shepherd replies.

Paxton nods with a big grin. "Let's do this."

"Since Dad is our investor, we need to make sure he agrees with it all. I'm sure he will, but until we pay back what he's invested, there's a lot at stake for him," Callum explains.

Imagine having a father who is not only supportive of your dreams, but actually puts his money in to make it a reality? Donald Atwood is that father. He's not my father, but I can't tell you the amount of times I've imagined he was.

Being a part of this makes me feel like I'm more of a son and brother than anything has before. It's something I will never take for granted and I will be grateful forever.

"This is all so exciting," Paxton says.

Callum nods. "Okay, let's go over positions."

Shepherd nods, and we all lean in closer.

"I'm now a master brewer and I've made a spreadsheet of what everyone can do. Obviously, Griffin will be our head chef." He glances at me and grins. "You ready for it, man?"

"Hell yes. It's the chance of a lifetime," I reply, excited to create my own menu.

"You could cook before, I can't imagine how much better it will be now," Paxton says.

I chuckle and lean back in the chair. "Just wait, you're gonna be blown away."

I'm not a cocky guy, but I am confident in my cooking. I've worked my ass off to get to where I am and while everything else in my life may be a mess, my cooking is flawless. I can't wait to create menus and show off all the new skills I've learned.

This brewery will have the best beer and the best food around. I have no doubt about that.

"Shep, we'll create beer recipes together and you'll be the one putting it all together in the barrels. Once Brock and Tripp are old enough, you can bring them in and teach them everything," Callum says.

That's the Atwood family motto, always being there for each other. While we are the ones getting the brewery up and running, Callum would never leave out his younger brothers. Even if they are just outside throwing the ball back and forth to each other right now, their futures are being taken care of.

It's kind of amazing.

"I can't wait to try some of these beer recipes I've been working on," Shepherd says with a nod.

"And Paxton, you'll go out and sell our beer. If anyone can do that, it's you." Callum says.

Paxton smiles, folding his hands on the table. "Believe me, I can sell anything to anyone."

This is it. This is the beginning of our future and it looks bright and successful.

"What about Anya?" Paxton asks.

Callum puts his spreadsheet back into the folder as he dips his eyebrows. "What about her?"

I look at Paxton, proud that he's looking out for his only sister. I wanted to ask, but it's not my place, but if Brock and Tripp have spots waiting for them, why wouldn't Anya?

"Well, aren't we going to offer her a job once she graduates? I mean she is our only sister," Paxton says.

Callum shakes his head as he stands up from the table. "She's going to school for interior design. Why would she even want to work at the brewery? She's got a successful future ahead of her."

For the next several minutes, we dive deep into discussing theme and design ideas for the brewery. We envision a hipster, old warehouse type of vibe, drawing inspiration from industrial aesthetics and vintage charm. The goal is to create an atmosphere that feels both trendy and timeless, appealing to a diverse crowd.

"Maybe some exposed brick walls?" Shepherd suggests.

We all nod.

"Love that idea, and I was thinking we could source materials from old barns or factories to maintain authenticity." Callum jots down his idea in his notebook.

"That's a great idea. I could even shop for ingredients at local farmer's markets," I say.

"We should definitely showcase some of the brewing equipment so customers can see where the beer is made," Paxton says.

"Definitely," Callum says, jotting down each idea as it comes. "Maybe get some local music on the weekends."

"Maybe we should have a huge chalkboard wall where customers can leave their names, or artwork," I say, loving the whole vibe of the brewery.

"That's a great idea," Shep says with a nod.

"I like the deep oranges, blood reds, and mustard yellows for the color schematics," Callum says, and we all agree.

"I can't wait to see the old power plant. Hopefully it has a few things leftover from when it was up and running," I say.

"For sure," Paxton says with a wide smile.

"I'll talk to Callum and get a day and time that we can all go tour the building. But, let's keep the work talk out of dinner since Anya is coming home for the first time," Shepherd says, getting up and going outside with his father and younger brothers.

"Anya's coming home?" I ask.

"Yeah, first time visiting since she left for college. Why do you think my mom is so happy?" Paxton asks.

Anya Atwood is the only girl in a slew of boys, and Carol is so grateful to have some estrogen among all the testosterone in the house. It must be hard for her being the only girl in the house now that Anya is gone.

"You look lost in thought," Callum says, slapping my shoulder as he comes back to the dining room. "Everything all right?"

I grin, nodding. This is my best friend. He's been there for me when no one else was. He might be a hard ass, but he's one of the kindest people I've ever met. He let me stay here countless times over the years without question. He knew I needed to get away and there was never any judgment, he just let me stay.

As for Carol and Don. They welcomed me into their home with smiles on their faces. That's just how they are. They love having a full house and welcome anyone at any time. Their door is never locked.

"This is it, man. All these years of talking about starting a brewery and it's really happening." Callum squeezes my shoulder as he grins. "I told you when you're focused and determined anything is possible."

"Hello?"

Callum jumps up as all the Atwood's rush to the front door at the sound of Anya's angelic voice.

"My baby girl," Carol says, rushing toward the front door with her arms outstretched.

Don and the boys are loudly talking and I hear a soft laugh drift around the corner. I can't see them, but I can hear the happiness in their voices. It makes me smile, just feeling like I'm a small part of it from another room.

Anya walks into the dining room and the wind is knocked out of me.

Holy fuck.

I haven't seen her since her freshman year of high school and wow how she's grown up. She's a knockout.

The tight shirt and jeans she's wearing show off her body, which up until right now I never would've noticed. But now I'm noticing, and I can't pull my eyes away.

She's always been pretty, but she's gorgeous now. Her big green eyes, full lips, and long brown hair, somehow seem matured, in the best possible way.

I stand up as she makes eye contact with me. "Anya, you've grown up," I say, wrapping her in a hug that is a little too tight and lasts a little too long.

"Hey, Griffin," she replies, almost like she's out of breath.

I force myself to let go of her, which is harder than it should be. My eyes run up and down her, which I swear causes her a chill. "How's school?"

"It's great. Couldn't love being away from all these boys more," she says, laughing as her brothers join us.

"Please, you miss us," Brock says, wrapping his arm around her.

I can't keep my eyes off her. It's impossible.

Even as we sit down for dinner, I can't help but constantly glance in her direction. I may even have laughed a little too hard at something she said, causing everyone to look at me. I played it off by coughing, but it was embarrassing.

"Mom, this meal is outstanding as always," Callum says.

"Truly, thank you again for having me," I say.

Carol smiles, waving my comment away. "You're always welcome, Griffin, you know that. No thanks needed."

"Boys, clear the table since your mother did all the cooking," Don says, grabbing a few plates.

All the Atwood boys and myself, get up and clear everything off the table.

Carol and Anya continue to sit at the table laughing as they talk. I don't even realize I'm staring until Callum slaps my shoulder.

"Griff, you good?"

I try to act unaffected as I look at him. "Never better. Can't stop thinking about the brewery."

He puts his arm around me and leads me into the living room, away from everyone. He sighs. "You sure about that? It seemed more like you couldn't stop thinking of Anya."

"What? No, come on. No, absolutely not," I say, tripping over my own words.

He lifts an eyebrow as he shakes his head. "You can date anyone you want, Griff. I'm always supportive. But my baby sister is off-limits. Starting this brewery, you're like family now. You get that, right?"

It feels like a knife to my chest, but I'll never admit it to anyone. It's just another secret I'll keep buried inside. "Of course, man. I would never cross that line."

He smiles and steps back out of my personal space. "Good."

But I don't feel good. In fact, I feel very, *very* bad.

Chapter 1

Anya
Present Day
Four Years Later

It's surreal being back from college and staying with my parents again. I flop onto my old bed, breathing in a deep breath. When I graduated college I had every plan in the world to go out on my own and make something of myself.

Interior design just wasn't for me, and it's why I changed my degree to business. Mainly Hospitality business, and I dream of the day I can be a part of Atta Boy Brewery and Restaurant.

I've been back for nearly five months now, and getting Callum to let me work at the brewery has been hard. He dismisses my ideas. Like they're nothing. He won't even listen to me when I tell him the back room of the restaurant isn't being utilized to its full potential.

Callum's always been sort of bossy. Especially to me. Maybe it's because he's the oldest, he feels he has the right to boss around the other Atwood siblings. Shepherd and Paxton are older than me, but don't treat me like I'm at their beck and call. However, Callum acts like a second father, always butting into my personal life, my professional life, just my life in general all the time.

It pisses me off. But when I evaluated the brewery on my own, I saw all this chance for future revenue potential. Private parties are a huge market. That room is just sitting there, empty. Not completely empty, it's got all the junk the boys toss in there when they can't be bothered to find a proper home for the stuff.

"Dinner's almost ready," my mother's voice rings from down-stairs, and I put on a bright pink lip gloss, fluff my brown curls in the mirror, and head downstairs.

Callum stops me at the bottom step. "Fine," he says in a gruff voice.

"Fine what?"

"Fine, I'm giving you six months to increase revenue with your private parties idea. You'll work hand-in-hand with Griffin. He knows, and he's ready to design menus for the parties."

I blink at my brother. He's gotten so tall since I've been away at college, and I wrap my arms around him. "You won't regret it," I tell him, happiness clear in my tone.

Griffin steps from around the corner, and I rush into his arms, squeezing him close to me. "Thank you," I tell him, even though he probably had nothing to do with making my brother see sense. I'm sure it was Paxton who finally convinced him.

Either way, I'm just so happy, and I don't think I've ever hugged Griffin before.

I step back, and his dark eyes bore into mine. "Um, you're welcome."

"I just told her she has been given carte blanche to do whatever she wants."

I spin around to smile at Callum. "I won't let you both down." I'm so excited. I skip away from my older brother and his best friend.

There's a knock at the door, and I swing it open and spot my best friend on the other side.

"Willow, I'm so glad you're here." I pull her inside. "Callum is letting me do private parties for Atta Boy."

Willow smiles, her long brown hair falling in waves down her back. "I'm happy for you, although I have told you a million times we'd love to have you over at Moore's."

Willow's family has owned Moore's Restaurant for as long as I can remember. Her grandfather started the fine dining steakhouse, and she works there as a front-of-the-house manager. She comes from a big family and is the only girl with five brothers to contend with. So, it's only normal that her and I would find each other and relate.

She's the sister I've always wanted.

We move through the house, and when she spots Griffin and Callum she stops.

"He really is so good-looking," Willow says, pushing me up the stairs. "Have you even noticed him since you've been back? He's single."

"Are you talking about Griffin?"

We move down the hallway and end up in my childhood bedroom. Willow and I spent many days and nights here, talking about boys, playing dolls, and trying on clothes.

"Do you like him?" I ask her, a feeling of jealousy washing over me momentarily. I don't even know where the jealousy comes from, but it's there, growing the more and more I think about Willow and Griffin together.

She makes a face of disgust. "Um no, I was thinking of him for you."

My eyes widen. "Griffin Cole and me?" The idea is planted, and I can't make heads or tails of it. Griffin Cole? I've never really thought of him in that way. I mean, sure, he's gorgeous, and there was a time when I saw him my freshman year of college that I thought maybe, but I haven't seen him since, and now it's just…I don't know.

Something I've never thought about.

"He's the head chef of Atta Boy, right?"

I blink. "You know he is."

Willow laughs. "You're going to be working with him a lot. A whole lot."

"Working. Nothing else."

Willow shrugs. "Fine. Is there anyone else you like? You've been home for nearly six months now. You have to have your sights set on somebody."

I shake my head. "Honestly, I haven't even thought about it. I've been so focused on getting my brother to see me as a serious contender to work at Atta Boy that I haven't even thought about dating."

Willow laughs. "I've got my eyes on like five different guys right now."

"Like who?"

"Well, I've been sort of talking to Lake Spriggs."

"Lake? As in one of Paxton's best friends?" I've known Lake Spriggs for years. He's been best friends with one of my brothers growing up. I haven't seen him in years either. I remember him though, blond hair, blue eyes.

I think about Willow and Lake together.

"Yes, him."

I smile. "I actually think you two would be perfect for each other. Well, from what I remember of him. He is so nice."

Willow has stars in her eyes as she smiles at me. "And so charming. I think he might be the one."

"Wow, the one, huh?"

"Dinner," my mother calls from downstairs, and Willow and I rise from my bed.

When we get downstairs there's only two chairs at the table left. Me sitting between Callum and Griffin, and Willow sitting between Brock and Tripp.

"Willow, nice to see you again," Brock says, passing the rolls her way.

"Thanks. I thought I should come and celebrate with Anya." Willow plops a roll onto her plate.

"Celebrate what?" Brock asks her.

"She just got a new job."

Brock's eyebrows raise, and he glances my way. "Oh yeah?"

Griffin clears his throat. "She's Atta Boy's newest event coordinator."

The table erupts into congratulatory praises as I blush.

"I knew Callum would come to his senses," Paxton says, and I give him a funny look.

"Aren't you the one who convinced him to give me a shot?"

Paxton shakes his head. "I mean, yeah I talked to him, but…"

His words are cut off from Griffin next to me who nudges me with his elbow. "I was the one. I thought it would be a good thing for the business."

I gaze up into Griffin's eyes as the rest of everyone chatters around the table. Only now it feels like just us two are sitting here. I'm nervous as I stare at him.

Maybe it's because of what Willow just said. Maybe it's because I never noticed how light-brown his eyes are with specks of green near the pupil. Maybe it's because I've never noticed just how good-looking Griffin is. Or how he looks at me like he wants to devour me. I'm not going to lie, it kind of turns me into a puddle of want.

"Thank you," I whisper so only he can hear me. And just like that the moment is broken when Willow and Brock start bickering back and forth over which restaurant has a better burger.

Chapter 2

Griffin

I flop down into bed and let out a groan. I'm exhausted. Today we were so busy and I've been on my feet since I woke up. It's now after two in the morning and I'm just lying down.

My thoughts drift to the conversation I had with Anya today. She's just starting to clear out the back room and get her thoughts together on what is going to happen in there. When I poked my head in to see how it was going she smiled at me and my pulse began to race. She said we need to sit down and get some ideas for the menu. A simple request, but damn the thought of sitting down with her does things to me that it shouldn't.

It's strange having her around all the time. I made a promise to Callum years ago that I would stay away from his sister and I will never break that promise, but I can't help that when I look at her she knocks the wind out of me.

I pushed Callum to let her do this and I'm not entirely sure why that was.

One thing is for sure though, it was either the smartest or dumbest thing I've ever done.

My phone vibrates on the nightstand and I groan reaching over to see who it is.

> Callum: My sister has just informed me that she booked a party for next weekend. This means we all need to get that room ready, plus you need to get with her and get a menu going.

> That was fast.

> Callum: A little too fast. We aren't close to ready. This is the shit I was afraid of.

Until she starts making serious money from this idea, Callum is going to be a hardass about it. Part of my job as his best friend is to try to get him to focus on the positive things. To make him understand not everything falls on his shoulders and that he needs to chill out sometimes.

It's not an easy job, but I try my best.

> She's selling her idea which will ultimately be beneficial to us all. We'll get the room ready in plenty of time and I'll carve out time to work on the menu with her. We've got this, C. It's an exciting new chapter for the brewery.

He takes a few minutes to reply and to anyone else, they would think he's just occupied with something else. But, I know better. He's dissecting everything I've just said and processing it. He's evaluating the pros and cons. He's detailing how much time and money this is all going to take to make happen in time.

Don't Fall For Your Brother's Best Friend

Like I said, my job as his best friend isn't easy.

Finally, my phone vibrates and I look at his reply.

> Callum: Yeah all right. I want everyone at the brewery an hour early to get a jump on that room.

I give him a thumb-up emoji and toss my phone back on the nightstand. An hour early means I have an hour less to sleep. Which sucks but there's no point in arguing with Callum. The man can survive a day with twenty minutes of sleep. He's a fucking machine.

<hr>

"Callum, what do you want to do with all these old receipts and orders?" Shepherd asks, holding one of the numerous boxes.

"I guess put all the boxes in my office and clutter it more than it already is." He pushes a chair against the table and looks around. "This is fucking ridiculous."

I grab his shoulder and he glances at me. "This is progress. You no longer use paper receipts or orders, so we'll scan all these into the computer in a file and you can get rid of the clutter. Don't overthink it, man."

Anya's eyes bounce between Callum and me while Paxton, Shepherd, and Tripp carry out the boxes.

He blows out a breath and nods. "Let's call it a night. We've been at this for hours."

"I appreciate it, Callum. I promise you won't regret this," Anya says, twisting her hands together.

19

"So you keep saying," he says, grabbing his phone off the table and walking out of the room.

She groans and knocks over a chair. "I'm so tired of his negative attitude."

I move toward her and pick up the chair before reaching out and touching her wrist. Her eyes snap to mine and I immediately let go. "You know how he is. It's going to take time, but he'll see what an amazing idea this is."

She searches my face and leans her hip against the table. "Why did you convince him to let me do this?"

I shrug and stuff my hands into my pockets. "It's a good idea, Anya. I'm able to see how much money can be made. Callum just takes a little longer to get there."

Her face lights up as a smile spreads across her kissable lips. "Thank you, again."

"So we need to carry all the boxes and you get to stay here doing what?" Tripp asks, pulling out a chair and sitting down.

"Anya and I are going to sit down and go over the menu for the party. You're more than welcome to go into the kitchen and be my sous chef instead," I say, grinning.

"There's an idea. Maybe you can get Tripp to stop complaining every five seconds that he's not on his damn phone," Paxton says, narrowing his eyes at his youngest brother.

Tripp rolls his eyes and stands up. "Not cool with being in the kitchen. What the hell do we need to do to get out of here?"

Everyone is exhausted and it's causing frustration that doesn't need to be here.

"Listen, Callum said we'll finish up tomorrow. You guys can get out of here," I say.

Tripp doesn't wait around, he rushes out the door with his phone in his hand.

"You aren't leaving?" Paxton asks, sitting on one of the tables.

"Anya and I need to discuss the menu. I promised Callum I'd get it done today."

Anya pulls out a chair and sits down. "This is supposed to be fun and exciting, but it's feeling forced and unwanted."

Shepherd wraps his arm around her shoulders as Paxton shakes his head. She's not wrong, it does feel that way.

"Come on baby sister, you know that's not true. I've been your advocate since you told me the idea. Don't let Callum and his bossy attitude get to you. You aren't new to his personality," Paxton says.

"He's right. We support this idea and we've got your back. It's exciting and you should let yourself feel the happiness you're trying to hide," Shepherd says.

She looks around at the three of us and forces a smile. "Thanks. I do appreciate all the help and support. It's been a long day. We should all just go get some sleep and start fresh tomorrow."

That's not gonna work for me, but she obviously needs a break.

"Good idea. I'll lock up," I say with a nod.

"Come on, Anya, I'll walk you to your car," Paxton says, jumping off the table.

"This room is going to be amazing. You'll see," Shepherd says, kissing the top of her head. He turns to me and nods. "You sure you don't mind locking up?"

I shake my head and follow them out of the room. "Yeah, I need to get a few things together for tomorrow. I'll be out of here in twenty minutes."

"Griffin, we'll go over the menu tomorrow if that's all right?" Anya appears exhausted, but still something in her eyes draws me in, making me want to wrap her into my arms.

"Don't worry about it. Just go get some rest," I say, waving as they walk toward the exit.

I head into the kitchen and get a few things ready for tomorrow. When that's done I grab a pen and paper. There's no way I'm waiting to figure out a menu. I'll get one together tonight at home. I know what she's going for and I know my ideas are going to surpass what she's thinking about anyway.

I turn everything off and lock up. As I'm walking to my Ford pickup truck, I realize I have a small grin on my face. As I climb into the truck I drop my head against the back of the seat. The idea of staying up late and doing this so that tomorrow Anya will be impressed is the reason I'm smiling.

Callum would kick my ass if he knew.

My phone beeps with a message before I even start my ignition.

> Tripp: Hey guys, Shepherd's got a new beer flavor he's been working on. Any guesses on what it is?

I text back.

> Knowing Shepherd, it's probably something weird like jalapeño and lime 😬

Callum: Nah, he did that one last year. I'm guessing it's something with fruit. Maybe a peach ale?

Brock: If it's as good as his last one, I'm in. When can we try it, Shepherd?

Shepherd: You guys are gonna love this one. It's a chocolate hazelnut porter.

Paxton: Ooh, sounds fancy. When can we get a taste?

Shepherd: How about this weekend? I need some guinea pigs to test it out before I finalize the recipe.

Tripp: Count me in. Anything with chocolate and beer is a win in my book.

First, Tripp, you're not old enough. And Shep, just to warn you, if it's bad, I'm gonna be brutally honest.

Shepherd: I wouldn't expect anything less from you, Griff.

Callum: Speaking of the weekend, anyone catch the game last night? That last-minute home run was insane!

Brock: Man, I thought they were done for. Best comeback I've seen in a while.

Paxton: I missed it! Had a busy night with Hartford, if you know what I mean. Any highlights worth watching?

Tripp: All of them! The whole game was intense. You gotta catch the replay.

Seriously, Paxton, it was one for the books. That last inning was pure magic.

Shepherd: I was so pumped, I almost knocked over the batch of beer I was working on.

Callum: Just make sure you don't spill any of that chocolate hazelnut goodness. We need to try it this weekend.

Paxton: All right, okay, I'll check out the highlights. And I'm definitely down for the beer tasting. What time?

Shepherd: How about Saturday afternoon? Say 3 PM at my place?

Tripp: Works for me. I can try beer, right, Cal?

Callum: I guess, don't tell Mom.

Brock: Perfect.

Callum: Can't wait.

Looking forward to it.

Paxton: See you guys then, and will your neighbor be there?

Shepherd: Don't remind me about her.

Callum: What happened?

Shepherd: She's back with her ex, so I guess I can go fuck myself.

Brock: Dude, sorry. It seemed like you really liked her.

Shepherd: Yeah, it's whatever.

Tripp: You need to make her jealous. Show her what she's missing.

Shepherd: Get a girlfriend, and maybe then I'll take dating advice from you.

Tripp: I've had girlfriends.

Callum: High school crushes don't count. Speaking of which, Brock, heard you're dating Millie. The Book, Spine, and Sinker book store owner.

Brock: Yeah, it's still new. So, no screwing it up for me.

Tripp: You're dating her?

Brock: Yeah. She's real nice.

Shepherd: You'll have to bring her to Sunday dinner.

Brock: Maybe I will.

I toss my phone onto the seat of my truck, and rub my eyes. Fuck, I need to get home.

Chapter 3

Anya

I forgot my notebook, so I turn my car around in the lot of Atta Boy, and park next to Griffin's truck. He's just about to leave, and I hop out.

He shuts off the ignition to his truck and steps out. "Forget something?"

"I'm glad you're still here. I thought I was going to have to wait until tomorrow to get my notebook." It really is ridiculous that Cal hasn't entrusted me with a key to the place yet, but I get it.

I'm an employee. Not an owner. This isn't my place.

Callum, Shep, Pax, and Griffin started this brewery with their own blood, sweat, and tears. I'm merely trying to enhance their vision.

Griffin opens the back door, and I follow him into the brewery. He shoves his hands into his pockets. "Do you really need the notebook tonight?"

I blush a little and together we walk through the brewery. "Busted," I say. "I wasn't planning on going home to sleep. I was actually going to think of ideas for the party this Friday."

Griffin offers a small laugh, and the sound of it vibrates through my bones. It sends chills skating down my spine. "I planned on doing the same thing. I was going home to work on the menu."

I feel horrible that Griffin is most likely exhausted from working all day, and helping us get the back room in order, and now he was planning on going home and working more. "You don't need to do that," I tell him.

He inches closer, and suddenly my mouth grows dry. I lick my lips, and for the first time since I've known Griffin, I realize how tall he is. How the top of my head would fit perfectly below his clavicle. That if he wrapped his strong arms around me it would probably make me feel just right. Or so I imagine.

What am I doing?

This is Griffin.

I should not be having these thoughts about him. I blame Willow for putting the idea in my head. For pointing out how good-looking he is. How have I never noticed before?

I mean, I've always known he's better looking than ninety percent of other men out there, but I have never noticed just how kind of gorgeous he is.

"I wanted to do it. I've got a lot of ideas."

I smile wide at the idea that Griffin is taking this project as seriously as me. It warms me up, making me feel all gooey inside.

Is that lame?

I know it is, but I can't help it. I'm happy to have his support, and apparently his attention. The way his eyes are laser-focused on me sends chills rushing over my skin. "What ideas?" I ask him, quietly.

His brown eyes darken momentarily, and I'd give anything in the world to know what he was thinking of at that very moment, but the second fades away and he pulls out a small notepad in his pocket. "I was thinking we could have three options. A filet option, grouper, and a vegetarian meal option. Maybe a pasta primavera."

"I think that's a great idea. It's a plated dinner for thirty people, so I want to make sure we pick things that won't kill your food costs."

Griffin raises a brow. "Let me worry about my food costs. I just want to make sure the guests are happy enough to tell their friends, and this private party thing works out."

"Thank you." I want to hug him. I want to fling my arms around his shoulders and squeeze him tight. However, I don't.

Griffin and I have never had that touchy-feely type of relationship. In fact, we don't really have anything, and I want to change all of that.

If we're going to be working together, I want to get to know him. He's practically an Atwood by association and I don't know much about him.

It's a shame, I think as I study his broad shoulders.

He takes off his chef's coat, and a tattoo peeks out from under the sleeve of his white shirt.

"Is that a tattoo?" I ask him, stepping closer to get a peek.

Griffin smiles, raising the sleeve of his shirt to showcase his artwork. "Yeah, got it a few years ago."

"Oh wow," I say, taking in the various chef's knives displayed in a design that wraps around his bicep. "I love it. You really love cooking, huh?"

Griffin drops his sleeve, letting it hide his tattoo, and leans against the railing of the stairs that lead up to the restaurant. "It was an escape for me growing up. I could take this handful of ingredients and create this masterpiece in the kitchen. It was almost like art."

"I burn toast," I admit to him.

"I'm sure that's not true."

I nod. "No, it is. I'm a disaster in the kitchen. During college I ate out for pretty much every meal. It's actually been kind of nice living back home and having my mother making home cooked meals every night."

"Yeah, your mother helped teach me how to cook a few things."

"Really? I never knew that."

When Griffin was most likely learning to cook at my house, I was probably busy playing with dolls in my room. Griffin's always been Callum's friend, and much older than me. But now, the four years spreading between us don't seem like much.

Griffin cracks a grin. "Yeah, I loved spending time at your house while I was in high school. It was like a second home."

He glances down at his feet. "A better home, anyway," he says under his breath.

I don't push for more of that info, just file it away for later, because there's one thing I'm certain of...I want to know more about this man.

"It's weird being home again."

"I bet. But I'm sure your mother loves having you there."

I beam. "She does. A little bit too much. She's trying to cook for me all the time. I don't think she ever wants me to leave. I would like to learn to cook."

Griffin pushes forward, standing to his full height. "I can teach you."

I shake my head. "No, you're already way too busy, and I really think you and I have our hands full with the parties. I'm not a complete mess in the kitchen. I do make chocolates."

Griffin studies me for a moment. "You make those?"

"What? Have you had some?"

"Yeah, Callum has given me some, saying they're from home. I figured your mother made them. I really like the raspberry-flavored ones."

"Those are my favorites too. And yes, I make them."

"Wow, I'm impressed. You should make them for the parties. Wrap them, and you can give them out at the end of the party. Or have them on the place setting for when they sit down."

"I never thought of that." I smile, loving the idea Griffin's come up with. I glance at my phone, noticing the time. "We should get going. It's late." I hate keeping Griffin late, because

I know he has to be back here bright and early tomorrow morning. I feel bad.

"Stay here. I'll run and get your notebook. What color is it?"

I shake my head. "No way." I rush up the stairs, and Griffin follows quickly behind. "I don't want you flipping through it."

He laughs. "Is it like a diary?"

I reach the landing, and make my way to the back of the restaurant to the room where the parties will be held. I swipe my pink notebook off the table and hug it close, breathing hard. "Maybe."

Griffin stands at the door, watching, waiting, leaning against the door jamb. A smirk graces his face, and he crosses his arms. "Now I'm intrigued."

"You're not going to read any of this." There's not much hidden in the pages of this silly notebook, but I love the way I've got his attention.

I walk closer to the door, and he takes up the whole of it. How will I get past him?

"Tell me one thing nobody else knows, and I'll let you pass," he says.

I blink up at him, thinking about what I could tell him. My heart races, and it's growing hot in here. "Umm, Willow told me that she thinks you're good-looking."

Griffin's eyes twitch ever so slightly, but I notice. "Willow's dating Lake. Try again."

"Okay, she did say it, but she said it because she thinks…" I can't believe I'm about to say this. "She thought you and I could date."

Griffin swallows, not saying anything, and I'm mortified.

I cut him off, wanting the awkwardness to disperse immediately. "But I told her that was crazy. You and I would never date." I laugh. "Could you imagine?" I ask, laughing more. I want to die. "Never never," I add on for good measure.

Griffin chuckles softly. "Yeah, never."

Chapter 4

Griffin

"Damn it, Tripp. I've had this burger up in the window for five minutes. Stop fucking around and get the food out when it's ready," I shout, wiping down the line.

He grabs the plate, mumbling under his breath, but rushes off when I snap my head and he sees my narrowed eyes.

"Chef, you all right?" Jared, my sous-chef asks.

That's a loaded question.

Everything is great. Anya's first party is tonight. The room we used to use for storage looks fantastic. She has tables set around with crisp white linens. There are candles on all of the tables and string lights hung around the room. The big window with a view of the courtyard is a feature now.

I busted my ass working on the menu to make sure it's perfect. We decided to go with filet, grouper, and a vegetarian pasta option. Everything has been delivered this morning and I'll be starting to prep soon.

The thing that has me snapping at everyone is something that really is a moot point. When Anya confessed that Willow said Anya and I should date, I felt something in my chest tighten. My pulse raced and for just a moment I allowed myself to imagine what that would be like. The idea of being able to do things to Anya that I've only fantasized about a handful of times had my skin overheating.

I stared at her, wanting her in that moment more than I wanted my next breath, and then she laughed. She repeated over and over how something like that would never happen and she laughed again.

It was a slap of reality to my face and to my cock.

I promised Callum years ago I would never date his sister. It's not something that will ever happen. Not even if Anya truly wanted it. I'd have to deny her.

I'm wondering if I could ever deny her anything.

My friendship and career would be put on the line and I can't lose them. So, the fact that I'm enraged about her laughing at the possibility is ridiculous.

Yet, here I am, days later still feeling it. Snapping at everyone and pushing down a fire that I haven't felt in a very long time. That fire, it isn't a good thing. It's something I felt growing up and I taught myself, with Callum's help, how to keep it smothered. I'm having trouble keeping it smothered now and that isn't helping my mood.

"Griff, everything good for tonight?" Shepherd asks, walking into the kitchen.

"All good. Jared and I are going to start prepping soon," I say, putting another burger on its bun.

He nods his head as he leans against the counter. The kitchen is crazy busy with the lunchtime rush, so my annoyance is getting poked with him standing there.

"The room looks awesome. I just helped Anya move some tables around. We even got the speakers working in there so there's light music playing now," he says, picking at a plate of fries I have sitting there.

"Shep, those are for someone, Christ," I say, shaking my head.

He laughs and grabs a couple more. "Tripp said you had a stick up your ass today. I guess he was right."

I turn to face him and cross my arms. "Tripp needs to deliver the food while it's still hot. If that's a problem, I must be doing my job wrong."

"What's really going on? You're never like this?" He raises a brow.

I shake my head and throw more fries in the fryer because he's still eating what I have prepared. "I'm busy, Shep, that's my problem. I'm trying to get through this lunch rush so I can focus on preparing for the party and then I need to cook that food and make sure the dinner rush is handled." I grab a brown disposable carton and toss the fries in it fresh from the fryer. "I just need to make sure everything is perfect, all right. It's the first night and I'm stressed out."

I need to get this fire under control. I'm better than this.

"I get it, man. I was really just checking in to make sure it wasn't anything else."

He doesn't know the extent of my life like Callum does, but he knows enough. It means the world to me that the Atwood brothers all care for me like I'm one of them.

I feel the fire fizzling out and I turn to him after dumping the new fries on the plate. "I'm sorry. I appreciate you checking in."

He grabs my shoulder and smiles. "Always, Griff, you know that."

I nod as the anger begins to smother. "I'll apologize to Tripp and Jared and Trudi."

We both laugh and I shake my head. I really have been out of control.

"You can apologize to Jared and Trudi, but not to Tripp. That little prick thinks he's a part owner lately. He needs to remember until he's older, he's an employee."

I remember being Tripp's age. He wants to grab the world by the balls while partying like it doesn't matter. Only he has a lot of expectations to live up to. It's got to be hard.

"If you need help with anything, give a shout. I'm going to help Brock clean out the still."

"Appreciate it," I shout as he walks out of the kitchen.

I close my eyes briefly and take a cleansing breath. My friendship with the Atwood's is everything. It's absurd thinking I let Anya's dismissal of a relationship get to me when, in fact, she's right—it'll never happen

⊏⊐

I plate the food for Anya's party. It's been a long day, but this moment makes it all worth it.

"Griffin, how's it going?" Anya asks, stepping into the kitchen. Her mere presence does something to me. Makes me almost feral. I need to remember to not be affected by her soft voice, and bright green eyes.

"It's going great in here. Everything will be ready in time, don't worry."

"Oh, I'm not worried. You're the only one who's been calm and collected through this entire thing," she says, tucking her brown hair behind her ears.

I chuckle and stand straight as I wipe my hands on a towel. "Maybe on the outside, but today wasn't my finest day."

"What do you mean?"

I lift my shoulders, taking in just how stunning she looks tonight. Her hair is down and curled. Her makeup makes her green eyes pop and shows off her full lips. The white button-down shirt she has on fits her body perfectly and she left the top two buttons undone, showing just enough cleavage to appear classy. The gray pencil skirt she has on makes you take notice of her long sexy legs. She looks professional and sexy, a killer combo.

"I took out my stress on Tripp," I admit.

She giggles, shaking her head. "He can handle it. He's the youngest, remember."

Not wanting to take away from her night, I just nod and move the conversation. "How's it going out there?"

She bites her lip and looks at the door leading out of the kitchen and back at me. "I don't want to jinx anything, but oh my God, it's going better than I ever imagined. Everyone is having a great time."

I can't fight the smile that takes over my face. "I knew it would be a success."

"I even saw Callum smiling," she says with a small laugh.

"Oh, you've crossed into uncharted territory, Anya. You should have a drink now to celebrate."

We both laugh and I hate that I need to get back to plating. Talking with her is so easy and fun.

Before I can say anything, Callum walks into the kitchen. My eyes lift to his and he looks between Anya and me. "What's going on?"

My brow dips as I stare at him. "Talking about the party," I say, slowly.

I feel like he's accusing me of something and I don't appreciate that. If he only knew what I've been talking myself out of lately, he'd feel like an asshole.

"Shouldn't you be out there?" he says directly to Anya.

"Shouldn't you be barking orders at Brock or Tripp? My party is going amazing and I'm allowed to come check in with my chef."

"Your chef?" Callum asks, raising an eyebrow.

She and I laugh as I get back to plating. "Callum, relax. You know what she means."

"As much as I'd love to stay, I do need to go check in with my servers," Anya says, walking out of the kitchen.

"Griff," Callum says. I turn my head and he crosses his arms. "Everything is good, right?"

I clear my throat and toss my rag on the counter. "You accusing me of something, Cal?"

"No, I'm definitely not."

"Feels like you are and if you feel the need to do that, maybe you don't feel the same about our friendship."

I turn my back on him and get back to work. He has no idea how hurtful his accusation is. Especially after everything I've been feeling.

"Griff, that's not true. You're like a brother to me. I'm sorry I even let myself think something like that. I know better. You'd never disrespect me or my family. Hell, you're a part of my family. I'm sorry, all right?"

I appreciate his apology, but it doesn't change the fact he let himself think I was untrustworthy with his sister.

"Yeah, okay. I need to get this done."

I hear his footsteps toward the door and he says, "She's my sister, Griff. I'm sorry."

I lift my head and pin him in my stare. "Exactly Callum, she's *your* sister."

He nods and walks out of the kitchen.

Well, two anomalies happened tonight. Anya saw Callum smile and I heard him apologize. Just the thought makes me laugh.

I step back and look at what I've plated and grin. Yep, this is going to blow them away.

I head back into the kitchen, leaning against the prep counter and pull out my phone.

> Saw something rare today.

> Brock: Let me guess, Mrs. Capri in a string bikini?

Tripp: That shit is not rare. She's old enough to be my grandmother, but she's rockin' a body on her.

Callum: Tripp, she's Mom's bestie. You're relentless. What did you see, Griff?

Callum actually smiled today.

Shepherd: Oh shit. Call in the papers. Did you snap a pic? That shit would go viral quick.

Callum: Ha ha ha.

Paxton: Seriously? I haven't seen a rare Callum smile in ages. Haven't seen a Shep smile in quite a while either.

Shepherd: Quoting the infamous words of Callum, 'ha ha ha'.

Tripp: Yeah Shep, what's up? We know why Callum doesn't smile, but what's your deal?

Callum: I smile.

Shepherd: No deal, just busy.

Paxton: Busy pouting about his neighbor. Just ask her out already.

Shepherd: She's back with that ex of hers, and I don't know.

Tripp: Ouch, sorry. It sucks when somebody you want is with someone else.

Shepherd: It's fine. I'm over it. So why did Callum smile?

Well, it was actually Anya who caught the smile, but I'm thinking Callum's finally seeing what we all see. That Anya kicks ass.

Paxton: Agreed.

Tripp: Yeah, she's okay.

Shepherd: She's rocking that party room hard.

Callum: We'll see.

And there you go, ruining it all. Gotta get back to work.

Chapter 5

Anya

I'm swimming with pride. Everything is going perfect, and the guests are having a great time. The food looks so good, that I'm sort of hoping Griffin made enough for me to have a few bites.

I giggle to myself thinking about eating some of the leftover food in the kitchen.

I'm sure grumpy Callum would never allow that.

The thing about Callum is he never goes away. He practically lives at Atta Boy. I mean, I get it, maybe I'd live here too if I had as much at stake as he does. He keeps things running. I just wish sometimes he'd let loose a bit.

But that'll never happen.

He's been like this since we were kids.

Bossy. Grumpy. An arrogant a-hole. There, I said it. Asshole.

I giggle to myself again, and realize I probably look like a psycho person standing in the corner of the room giggling while a private party is going on.

It's Clara Workman's 60th birthday party, and she's got all the book club members, their families, and her own personal friends here. It's a small intimate group, but they're having a great time.

I step over to where Clara is finishing up her pistachio-crusted grouper. "How's everything?" I ask her.

She wraps her hand around my arm, gazing up at me with unshed tears in her eyes. "Better than I ever could have imagined. I couldn't ask for a lovelier evening. Did you see Myrtle even showed?" She glances across the room, and we both smile over at Myrtle who is sitting at another table.

"She even looks happy," I say with a grin, and quickly add, "Everyone looks happy."

"Everyone is happy. It's all because of you. Harold and I love this place. Been coming since it opened, and I think it's great you all now offer private parties. Our 30th is coming up soon, we might book something."

I smile at Harold who sits next to her. "We'd love to host it for you."

"Thank you, dear."

I step away so they can enjoy the rest of their meal, and walk around to make sure everyone is doing okay.

Even Myrtle laughs. She's always been the grumpy old lady who lives across town and never comes out of her house, except to go to church on Sundays. It's almost sad if you think about it. Story is, she worked her whole life for some big company in New York, and never married. Never had any kids. Worked until she finally snapped one day and decided to move to a small town and relax. Maybe one day she'll enjoy her retirement, and meet somebody new.

I continue crossing the floor, and step over to where a few servers fill bus tubs with dirty dishes to take to the back. "I think once we get all the dinner plates up, we can serve dessert and then we can turn the music up a bit in case anyone wants to dance," I say to Gabby.

She nods, and then steps closer. "Did you see Mr. Charleston talking to Myrtle?" Gabby's worked at the restaurant for a few months, and is fresh out of high school, working until she leaves for college in the fall.

I snap my eyes to Myrtle, and sure enough Mr. Charleston is chatting away happily with her. "Do I hear wedding bells," I say with a laugh.

"I thought he always had a thing for Hartford's Aunt Nora," Tripp says, grabbing the bus tub of dishes to bring to the back of the house.

I shake my head. "I don't know."

Before Tripp heads into the kitchen, he smiles. "He's a player. He's got a woman in Florida, and now he'll have a woman here in Magnolia Ridge."

Gabby and I laugh as Tripp leaves. Another server by the name of Patrick steps over.

"Everyone's water is filled, and I'm grabbing a few drinks at the bar," he says.

"Okay, perfect. Thank you both so much," I say, happy that they're doing such a great job.

Callum strides back into the room, his footsteps echoing softly against the hardwood floors. With long strides, he navigates through the room until he stands before me. "Great party," he remarks, a weary smile tugging at the corners of his lips. "I'm heading up to my office if you need anything."

Feeling a pang of concern, I reach out and gently lay my hand on his bicep, the fabric of his suit jacket smooth beneath my touch. "Callum, everything is under control. Why don't you go home? You've been working tirelessly, and you're clearly exhausted. We can handle things from here," I offer, mustering my most reassuring smile.

"I'm fine," he insists, his voice gruffer than usual. But his facade crumbles under closer scrutiny. The lines etched in his face speak volumes with how little sleep he's actually getting, and his eyes have lost their glossy shine.

He's tired.

Anyone can see it.

"You're not fine," I tell him, softly.

"Maybe I can head out. Shep is here if you need anything, and I know Griffin is going to stay until the end of the party."

"Oh, he doesn't have to do that." Normally chefs leave once the last dessert has been served. "He can go."

Callum digs his phone out of his pocket, glancing at it momentarily before answering, "He doesn't mind. Okay, I need to call Paxton before I head out. Call me if anything comes up. I can be here quick."

"We'll be fine." I pretend to roll my eyes at him, letting him know he's being overly bossy.

As soon as he leaves I head back into the kitchen to look for the birthday cake.

"I'm going to take the cake out on this table with wheels, and everyone can sing happy birthday, and then we'll bring it back here and cut it," I say to Patrick and Gabby.

Griffin steps closer. "I also made some tarts, chocolate covered strawberries, and mini cannolis. You can set two plates on each table."

I look at the plates of dessert. "They look amazing."

Griffin raises a brow. "Next party you should make your own chocolates to serve."

My chest warms that Griffin even thought of this. I have to admit, I've had a few thoughts about serving my own chocolates at parties, but didn't want to assume anything. What if Callum hated the idea?

"Thanks," I tell him, and then for the rest of the party, we're a mad rush of dishing out birthday cake, clearing plates, serving coffee, and making sure the guests have a great time.

Once the party is over, and the last guests have left, Gabby and Patrick finish cleaning, and I head into the kitchen.

"How was it?" Griffin asks, the party ending way after the restaurant has closed.

So, Griffin's the only one around.

"It went great." I'm holding the finalized receipt of the bill, and smile. "The party brought in an extra five-thousand of revenue."

Griffin takes off his chef coat, and I laugh a little when I see the t-shirt he's wearing underneath. There's two kitchen knives crossing with the words, *'Nobody's better with their hands than a chef'* scrawled across the front.

It makes my mind wander. Is he good with his hands? Would he know just where to touch me? How to touch me?

Griffin notices the silence stretching between us, and sets his chef's coat down on the stainless steel prep table. "Everything okay?"

I'm sitting here gawking at him, and I realize I need to close my mouth. I snap it shut, and smile. "Everything's perfect. I should make sure Patrick and Gabby make it out okay."

"I can walk everyone to their cars."

"That's okay. Patrick can walk Gabby to her car. I'm going to input the numbers into the computer, but let me check on them first, make sure they got everything done."

"I'll be here," he whispers in a throaty growl, and it makes my body tingle.

I'm not even sure why. It wasn't anything sexual.

I head back into the event room to make sure Gabby and Patrick are all done, once they leave I make my way back to Griffin.

"Why don't you do the numbers tomorrow? It's late," he says.

"Are you kidding? I don't want to give my brother any ammunition for not keeping this event room going. Besides, I want him to come in first thing tomorrow morning and see the sales the party made."

Griffin laughs. "You know that mother fucker checks the sales from an app from his phone. He's probably sitting in bed right now, waiting on the numbers."

"Knowing Cal, you're probably right."

Griffin runs his hand along the stainless steel. "It's kind of sad, isn't it?"

"What?"

Griffin moves an inch closer. "Being all alone. Callum's never had anyone. He's lying in bed all alone. I'm guessing it gets lonely."

"Well, you're alone. I don't think you've ever even dated anyone." I try to recall if he's ever brought a girl around.

"A few girls here and there. Nothing serious. But Callum doesn't even go out and have fun."

"Do you have fun?" And by fun does he mean sleep around? Is Griffin a player? Like Tripp said about Mr. Charleston. A woman in Florida. A woman here. Does Griffin have women all across the country?

Stop.

That's ridiculous. Griffin is a nice guy. A complete cinnamon roll. He's not the type to play around. I think.

I don't know him that well, but what I do know is he isn't that guy.

He shakes his head and his brown eyes bore into mine. "I guess I don't have fun either." He lets out a tiny laugh. "Callum and I are more alike than I thought."

"You and Cal are nothing alike. He's all work all the time. I'm sure you have days off and have fun."

He raises his eyes to stare at the ceiling before settling back on me. "Honestly…"

My eyes widen. "Oh my god, Griffin. Do you not have fun on your days off?"

"What's a day off?"

"Griffin," I nearly yell. "You need to take some time off. You can't work twenty-four seven. It's not healthy. What do you like to do?" I ask him.

He shrugs. "Besides cooking?"

I crack a grin. "Yes, besides cooking."

"Umm, I guess I like to play golf sometimes."

I twist my nose up at the notion. "Not golf. That's boring. Why don't you, me, and Callum go do something on your next day off. Something fun."

He blinks at me.

"As friends," I rush out, not wanting him to get the wrong impression. "You both need to add some excitement into your lives, and I'm just the girl who can do that. I have Tuesday off next week. Do you think Callum can get the day off? Can you?"

Griffin smiles. "Callum can take off any day he wants. He's the boss, and yes I can take that day off too."

"Great, then it's settled. We'll go blow off some steam."

What am I asking him to do? Is this wise? He's been a family friend for years, and for some reason, the thought of him sitting at home all alone does something to my insides. Makes my chest clench. A sadness grows. I want to help him in some small way.

I have no idea what we'll do, but that doesn't stop me from saying, "Leave it to me. I'll plan everything."

Chapter 6

Griffin

I slip my shirt on and look in the mirror. A sigh escapes me as I pull it off, tossing it on the bed. I can't hang out with Anya wearing a shirt that says '*Let Me Hear You Say Yes Chef.*' To play it safe, I pull out a navy blue plain t-shirt.

Today Anya, Callum, and I are supposed to go have fun. She hasn't told either of us what the fun is, but I guess that's supposed to be part of the fun. I have no idea.

Honestly, until Anya pointed out that I don't have fun, I really didn't notice. For me, cooking is fun. It's my release. So, it never occurred to me that I should be doing other things.

I've given some thought to what Anya was saying about Callum feeling lonely. It struck a chord with me because he's the reason I wasn't lonely for most of my life. No one should feel lonely.

My phone alerts me and I grab it off my dresser as I leave my bedroom.

Paxton: Thanks for the invite today.

Callum: You can come and I'll go into work.

Pax, come with us.

Brock: What did I miss?

I chuckle, grabbing a water out of the fridge. The Atwood boys love teasing each other. It's always fun, whether I'm just listening or jumping in myself. I glance at the group chat, and see it's the one with Anya in it, not just us guys.

Paxton: Anya invited Callum and Griffin for a day of fun. I guess she doesn't care if we get to have fun.

Anya: Stop it. I'd never exclude anyone. Callum and Griffin need help having fun. You guys don't.

Brock: Oh burn lol

Callum: I don't need help having fun. I have plenty of fun.

No you don't and neither do I. Anya is right, we need help.

Brock: If you guys want to have fun, you should be asking me, not Anya.

Anya: Hookers are not fun.

Paxton: Your girlfriend dressing up like one is.

Anya: Gross.

Brock: Nice.

Callum: Too much information.

...

Paxton: Speechless, Griff?

Not exactly the image I need next time I see Hartford.

Brock: Stop getting sidetracked. What's this day of fun we were cut out of?

No idea.

Paxton: Oh shit, that would make me nervous. Anya in charge with no information. Good luck guys, I definitely don't want in on this.

I laugh, but suddenly I wonder if I should be nervous. What could she have planned? I'll be honest, I'm glad Callum is gonna be there.

Brock: One time Anya told me she had something fun planned and I had to end up taking her to the mall so she could hang out with Willow. And we all know I hate hanging out with Willow.

Callum: Anya Marie Atwood, I need details of what you have planned, or I'm going to work.

> Anya: Wow, Brock. The mall was your idea, remember? You had a crush on some girl at the Sephora store. Callum, I'm taking you and Griffin to do ax throwing. Now can everyone stop texting so I can finish getting ready?

Ax throwing does sound kinda fun.

———

Callum picks me up and we arrive at Ax Attack. I never even noticed this place before and I drive by it almost every day.

"You ever been here?" I ask, looking up at the sign.

He looks at me and raises an eyebrow. "Seriously?"

I laugh and slap his arm. "Come on, throwing an ax is probably therapeutic."

"Working is therapeutic," he huffs.

I shake my head and open my door. "We need to learn how to have fun that doesn't include work."

He climbs out and we meet in front of his truck. "We were both content until Anya said differently."

I think about that for a minute. He's right. Until Anya said something it never occurred to me and now it's all I think about. I don't want to be a boring guy who dedicates his entire life to work. The thought of waking up one day, alone, is starting to become a thought that I can't handle because it happens. Look at Myrtle.

"I think she just brought to light what we've been denying."

It's what I want to believe, anyway.

"She's a pushy little thing. Being the only girl she isn't used to hearing the word no."

He shoves his hands into his pockets and I chuckle. He looks at me, lifting an eyebrow.

"Sorry, but I think if she's not used to hearing the word no, it's because she learned it from her oldest brother."

"I hear that word all the time," he argues.

"Maybe, but you never accept it."

A small grin hits his lips as he nods. "True."

"You guys beat me here. Must mean you're excited," Anya says, smiling as she looks between us.

My heart slams against my chest when her eyes connect with mine. The wind is knocked out of me as her smile grows bigger.

She looks beautiful.

Her hair is down, framing her face. Her makeup is a bit heavier than normal, giving her a sexy look. The tight jeans she's wearing are paired with a pink and black flannel that is unbuttoned with a black tank top underneath, making my dick take notice. Which is not a good thing.

"Yeah, as excited as I get going to the dentist," Callum says, snapping me out of my eye-fucking of his sister.

Fuck. I'm eye-fucking his sister.

Anya laughs and it vibrates through me as I try to collect myself.

"Let's go, you're going to love this," she says, pulling on his arm.

We walk through the door and I'm not sure what I imagined, but it wasn't this. It's a really cool setup. The entire place has a woodsy feel with lots of wood and string lights throughout. I'm also surprised at the vast variety of people playing.

There are couples who you can tell are on a date. Families with older children. Large groups and small groups. It's pretty intriguing.

We are brought to our area and I look around. There's what I can only describe as fencing separating the areas all the way to the ceiling. The back wall has two large wooden targets that are on a dark-wooden wall.

"Do not pass this line," the employee explains. He's an older kid, probably sixteen, or seventeen with a big mustache and a mullet. I think he's a Collins kid. They just recently moved to town, but I haven't met any of them yet. His name tag reads 'Freddie.'

I glance at the line, but as he continues to go over the rules my attention goes to the couple next to us. They are clearly on a date and I watch as she jumps into his arms after throwing her ax. They look so happy and I feel a ping of jealousy.

A happy couple isn't something I saw much of until I found the Atwoods. You can clearly see the love Mr. Atwood has for his wife. Hell, even how Paxton looks at Hartford. Everyone knew how much he'd always liked her, and now they're together.

"Here's your axes," Freddie says.

I turn my head and notice Anya staring at me. She tilts her head, curious as to what held my attention. Not willing to have any kind of discussion about it, I just smile and grab my ax.

"This is heavier than I expected," Anya says.

"It's an ax, Anya. What did you think it would feel like?" Callum asks.

I never really noticed how Callum belittles her, but recently I've been paying closer attention. He treats her like she's still a child sometimes, which couldn't be further from the truth. I don't even think Anya notices and if she does, it doesn't appear to bother her.

I wish I could say the same.

It bothers the fuck out of me. I don't view her as a child. I definitely don't view her as a little sister.

"It's a hell of a lot heavier than my knives, that's for sure," I say.

Anya laughs, while Callum shakes his head.

"I'm going first," Anya says, excitedly, walking up to the line.

"She's going to drop it. Don't stand behind her," Callum whispers, pulling me aside.

I stare at her, hoping she proves her brother wrong.

She has a tight grip on the handle with both hands and brings it behind her head. My stomach tightens with worry that she'll hurt herself. But she swings her arms forward and lets the ax fly. She's so excited, but it quickly fades as the ax falls before reaching the target.

"Damn," she says, turning around to face us.

"Nice try, little sister. Now watch how it's done."

She rolls her eyes, but laughs as Callum walks to the line. He throws his ax and it hits the top corner, just making it onto the target. He turns around smiling as he points to his shot.

"Beat that," he says, wrapping his arm around his sister.

I don't say anything as I step up to the line. I crack my neck and he chuckles behind me. He can laugh, but I'm about to show him how it's done. I wrap my hands around the ax and bring it behind my head. I allow my hands to slide down the handle a bit as I swing my arms forward. I let go and watch as the ax hits incredibly close to the bullseye.

"Holy wow," Anya says behind me.

"Beginners luck," Callum replies.

I turn around smiling as I point to the ax. "Now beat that."

We all laugh and now I understand why Anya chose this. Callum and I, hell all of the Atwoods, are all extremely competitive. She knew this would turn into just that and Callum and I would have a blast.

Which is exactly what happens.

Callum starts to take each throw more serious than the last. I can't help laughing each time I beat him, which pisses him off. Anya is still struggling, but every time I try to give advice, Callum just yells to throw it.

Anya steps up for her throw and Callum gets a phone call. "I need to take this," he says, walking away.

I watch him go outside before I turn to Anya. "Hey, wait," I say, stepping next to her.

She lowers her arms, now holding the ax with one hand. "What?"

"You're holding the ax wrong." I grab the handle of her ax, pulling it up while her one hand is still on it. "Wrap both hands around the handle." She does and I nod. "Good, but see how high up you have them, you need to move them down." She does, but not far enough, so I step behind her, wrapping my arms around her to reach her hands. I cover her hands with one of mine and move them down the ax. "Hold it here," I whisper, entirely too close to her. I can smell her sweet coconut scent and feel her body heat radiating onto me.

"Like this?" she asks, her voice soft.

"Just like that. Now when you bring your arms back, put all your force behind it and let go after you can see the ax. Keep your eyes on the bullseye. You can do this, Anya."

My breathing has increased, just as hers has. I feel a fire burning inside me, but it's different than normal. It's not trying to eat me alive. It's a feeling of excitement.

I step back, reluctantly, and when her eyes find mine, I smile and nod.

She does exactly what I say and her ax hits the target and sticks.

"Oh my God, I did it." She turns around, the pride and excitement beaming off of her is infectious. "Griffin, I did it." She runs and jumps at me and I catch her, wrapping my arms around her small body. Her arms cling to me tightly and we fall silent.

The excitement quickly turns into something else and I'd be lying if I said I didn't like it. She feels good in my arms. Like she belongs.

I can feel her warm breath on my neck and it's like a shock against my skin. A soft sigh escapes her and I close my eyes, soaking it all in.

"Thank you," she whispers.

"You did great, Anya."

I tighten my hold briefly before I let her go.

I don't want to let her go and that's exactly why I do it.

She smiles up at me, a small blush on her cheeks as she straightens her flannel shirt. Our eyes are locked and she opens her mouth to say something, but Callum interrupts.

"You guys almost ready? It's fun and all, but I wanna pop in the brewery before it closes," he says, looking between us.

I clear my throat and nod. "Yeah, let's just go a couple more times. I think Anya would like that."

"Yeah, okay fine."

We spend another half hour throwing and Anya hits the target each time. She never gets a bullseye, but her excitement each time she hits it feels like she does.

I was reluctant to go out tonight, but as we get ready to leave, I don't want to. I want this fire that started before to continue to burn and I know when we leave, it will extinguish.

"I told you guys it would be fun," she says as we walk outside.

"It was all right. Not something I want to do all the time," Callum says.

I grin as I bump my shoulder to hers. "It was fun and I would do it again."

And again and again. As long as she's there too.

If she offers another night of fun, I'm all in.

Chapter 7

Anya

"They look great, dear," my mother says as I pop the last of the chocolates out of the heart molds.

"Do they?" I ask her, tilting my head to give them a better inspection. "I'm hoping they'll be good enough for an anniversary dinner I'm hosting tonight at the brewery."

My mother beams. "I love that you're working there. You're such a smart woman." My mother brushes my hair out of my face.

"I just wish Callum would see that."

My mother steps back, leaning against the kitchen counter. We've been making chocolate candies all day for the event tonight. "He will. How was the axe throwing with him?"

I think back to the other night when Griffin wrapped his arms around me to show me how to grip the axe. Shivers wrack my body at the memory, and thankfully my mother was looking the other way, snagging a chocolate off the plate and popping it into her mouth.

I smile wide. "I saw that," I say, with a raise of my brow.

"So, how was it?" my mother asks again.

"It was fun. Callum and Griffin even smiled a few times." I laugh at remembering the two of them competing.

"That's good. I'm glad you brought Griffin along." My mother snatches another chocolate and pops it into her mouth.

"Mom?" I park both hands on my hips. "I'm not going to have any left for the party."

My mother laughs. "Is Griffin working the party?"

I spin around to continue working on the chocolates as I shrug. "I guess. He works all the parties."

"I think he has a little thing for you," my mother says, and I turn back around to meet her eyes. She winks, and smiles wide. "I think he's always had a little thing for you, Anya."

I shake my head. "No way." Has he? Has he always had a crush?

No, I would know if Griffin were harboring feelings for me, and he's definitely not. He's like a…my thought falls away as I try to think of the perfect word for Griffin. He's not like an older brother. No way. He's much too good-looking and hot to be a brother. Not saying my brothers are ugly, but gross, they're my brothers.

I don't view Griffin like that.

Is he a friend?

I mean, I guess you could call him a friend. Even though we've never really hung out except for the other night with the axe throwing.

"Pretty soon smoke is going to come out of your ears," my mother says.

I glance up, lost in thought. "What?"

"What are you thinking about?"

I shake my head. "He doesn't have a crush. We're friends."

My mother grabs another chocolate and pops it into her mouth, and utters the word "good," as she walks out of the kitchen.

I glance at my phone and notice the time.

I'm going to be late.

I rush around the house, getting dressed and getting the chocolates packed up so I can transport them to the brewery. On my way, I think about what my mother said. If it's true, then how do I feel about him?

I mean, he's Griffin. I've always thought he was gorgeous, but that's all it's ever been.

A warmth washes over me as I think about his arms around me. The way he spoke low in my ear. There's just something about him.

As I park in the back of the brewery, I pull out my handbag and chocolates.

"Hey, Anya," Brock says, hosing the back area.

"Hey, what's up?" I step closer to my younger brother with a big smile.

"Just cleaning up. I have Mr. Daniels picking up the spent grain for his horses soon, so I'm waiting out here for that."

"Speak of the devil," I say as I spot Mr. Daniels' red truck pull up.

Mr. Daniels hops out of his truck. "Anya, haven't seen you in ages. What have you been up to?"

I shrug. "Working here now."

Mr. Daniels shifts his trucker cap on his head as he smiles. "Ah, that's good. I'm just here to pick up the grain for the horses."

I nod. It's so great that Callum offered to give the spent grain that's leftover for Mr. Daniels to take home for free. Even though Callum comes off as a hard ass, I know he has a heart deep inside his rough exterior. "How are the horses?"

"They're good. You haven't been out in ages to ride."

I used to ride every weekend while in high school, but since I've been back from college I haven't had time to get back out there. "Actually," I say, an idea forming. "Would I be able to bring Callum and Griffin with me to come riding?"

Mr. Daniels smiles. "Sure, just let me know what day you want to come up."

"What about me?" Brock says, obviously feeling left out.

"You hate horses," I say with a laugh.

He sets the hose down. "I would just like to be included so I can politely decline."

I laugh harder. "Okay, Mr. Daniels, can Griffin, Callum, me, *and Brock* come ride?"

Mr. Daniels shifts his hat on his head once more. "Sure thing."

Brock tilts his head. "Ah, sorry I can't make it. Sorry."

We all laugh as Brock grabs the bags of spent to help Mr. Daniels load it into his truck. I say my goodbyes, walking into the brewery.

I can't wait to tell Callum and Griffin we're going to ride horses for fun next, but first I need to make sure this party goes off without a hitch.

⊏⊐

"Horses?" Callum says with a twist of his face. "I haven't rode a horse since I was a kid. I doubt I even know how anymore."

"It's like riding a bike," I say, sitting on the top of Callum's desk in his office.

He's standing behind his desk where I found him on my down time during my party. The anniversary dinner has been a success, and now we're just waiting on the party to wrap up before we can do the paperwork and go home.

Griffin's been in the kitchen, cleaning things up, and I'm sure he's already left. Things between us were normal tonight. I tried to look for any signs that he might possibly have a crush, but so far I've seen nothing.

"Callum," Griffin says, walking into the office. Once he spots me on the desk, he freezes. "Oh, hi Anya."

I slide off the desk. "Hey, glad you're here. We're going horse-back riding."

He steps further into the room. "Excuse me?"

I laugh lightly at the confusion all over his handsome face. Wow, he really is quite good-looking. I mean, more than usual. Which is saying something. "Horses. It'll be fun."

Callum huffs audibly as he folds his arms, dragging our attention to him. "Anya thinks riding horses on a farm will be fun."

Griffin rubs a hand on the back of his neck. "I'm down."

"Great." I walk past him. "I need to check on things upstairs," I say, glancing over my shoulder.

As I head upstairs to the room, I laugh silently to myself. I can't wait to see them both on horses. Oh wait.

I stall. Griffin on a horse? My eyes widen at the images flashing through my mind. Griffin with no shirt on, jeans, and a cowboy hat. His thick thighs working as he rides the horse, his body moving up and down.

This might be a bad idea.

"What are you doing?" Griffin's voice comes up behind me as I turn around.

"I was headed to the party room," I say, hoping he didn't see me standing on the staircase.

"Callum's not too happy about the horses."

I wave Griffin off. "Callum wasn't too happy about the axe throwing either, but he survived." I smile.

Griffin steps closer, to where we're face to face. "He barely survived. I...uh, barely survived too."

"Was it that horrible?"

A smile splits his face. "Quite the opposite actually." And then Griffin brushes past me as he continues up the stairs to the kitchen.

I suck in a deep breath, needing oxygen more than anything. What did he mean by that? Does Griffin have a crush on me?

Me?

He could have any woman in the world he wants. Why would he be crushing on me?

I continue up the stairs after him, rushing into the room to check on the party.

"The chocolates were a hit," Patrick says as he clears a few tables.

"When did they leave?" I ask, upset with myself that I was too busy worrying about Griffin than knowing when my party left the building.

"Like five minutes ago. They had a great time."

Phew.

"Good."

I help Patrick and a few of the other servers break down the place for the night. It's late once I've finished the paperwork, and when I turn out the lights to leave, Griffin is by the back door.

"I'll walk you out," he says.

I glance up at him. "What are you still doing here?"

He steps closer, and I suck in a breath. "Someone has to walk you out. It's not safe."

"My car is really close." I can't turn my eyes away from his. They're this light brown color, and it makes me want to lean in and see if I can pinpoint where the iris ends and the pupil begins.

"Then I don't have to walk you as far." He offers a small laugh, and the sound reverberates through my body, making my nipples pebble.

What is happening to me?

I almost want him to kiss me. But that's an absurd thought. Isn't it?

I blink at him, and shake my head slightly to break myself from this spell that has fallen over me. "You didn't have to stay late just for me. I feel bad," I say to him.

"I'd never be able to live with myself if anything happened to you."

My chest squeezes tight at his words, and I want to kiss him. So, feeling brave, I lean in, rest my hand on his bicep and close my eyes.

"Anya," he whispers. "What are you doing?" He steps back, and oh my god.

I slide my eyes open slowly, and Griffin stares at me like I've grown two heads. And I am *mortified*.

Without a word, I rush out of the back door and hurry to my car.

"Anya, wait," Griffin says behind me, but I don't turn back.

I'm humiliated.

I let my mother get in my head. *'He has a crush.'*

Stupid Anya.

There's no silly crush. There's nothing.

I feel like a dang fool.

Chapter 8

Griffin

I stand there watching Anya's tail lights, feeling like an asshole. She put herself out there. Put her feelings on the line and I crushed them.

My head falls back as I scrub my face. I had no idea she was attracted to me. Which makes this that much worse. If she wasn't Callum's sister, I would've slammed my lips to hers. I would've pulled her against me, sinking my fingers into her hair while I deepened the kiss. She would've had no doubt about how I feel about her.

But, she *is* Callum's sister and I made a promise that I can *not* break.

I climb into my truck and once the door is closed I slam my hands against the steering wheel. "Fuck."

As I drive home the image of Anya leaning in to kiss me plays over and over in my head. My anger rises. I'm pissed at myself for denying her. I'm pissed at Callum for making me promise something I now regret.

Another man, a better man, would have followed her home and tried to explain himself. But as I pull into my driveway, I shake my head. Even if I was that man, what could I say? I can't tell her that her brother has put her in the off-limits category. I can't tell her that not kissing her back is something that will haunt me for the rest of my life. The only thing I could do is lie and tell her I don't feel that way about her and I'm sure she'd see the sham in my eyes.

My mother didn't teach me much, but she always told me not to lie. Which is a fucking joke because her entire life was a lie.

I grab a Kunt Kicker IPA out of the fridge and sit down on my dark navy couch. After taking a long pull, I sigh, closing my eyes. I make it a point to block out as much of my childhood as possible, but feeling like I've hurt Anya, makes it impossible to keep those times pushed down.

Growing up in my house was the equivalent of walking around a minefield. One misstep and everything would blow up.

Ever heard the saying 'walking on eggshells?' Well my life was walking on the whole damn egg, a mess no matter which way you saw it.

My father was an angry man, a storm always on the horizon. If he wasn't happy, no one was happy. A loud child running around laughing wasn't something he appreciated. He didn't like a messy house. Toys scattered on the floor, and snacks left on the table, were just unacceptable to him. He liked silence. He liked order. Things that a child doesn't give you. Every noise, every cluttered space was an affront to his need for control and tranquility.

My mother catered to him, making sure he got everything he wanted. I couldn't be loud, I couldn't make a mess, I couldn't be a kid. I remember tiptoeing around the house, holding my breath, hoping not to disturb the fragile peace. I couldn't laugh freely, couldn't let my imagination spill into my surroundings. I couldn't be happy.

I'm not entirely sure when my father started cheating on my mother, but it happened. Perhaps it was inevitable. I'm sure he liked the idea of pretending he didn't have a wife and kid at home, responsibilities that he felt shackled by. He was always chasing after younger women, women with no kids, women who represented the freedom and adoration he craved. It was his way of escaping the life he resented.

My mother just pretended none of it was happening. The cheating, the way he treated me, the way he treated her. She walked about this town smiling and lying about what a great life she had. She wore her denial like a mask, plastering over the cracks in our family's façade. I would watch her, wondering how she could smile while our world was crumbling, how she could act as if everything was fine while I felt suffocated by the tension and sadness. Her pretense was a survival tactic, a desperate attempt to keep our fractured lives from falling apart completely.

You'd think with his wandering dick, clean house, quiet child, and a wife that was at his beck and call it would make him happy.

It didn't.

He was still a miserable prick. I spent far too much time hiding in my room, afraid of what I might get in trouble for. One time I brought a couple of little cars out to the living room while he was out fucking someone. It was the most fun. I drove those little cars all over the place. The living room was so much bigger than my bedroom, and I remember I even laughed a few times when the cars sped across the floor, their tiny wheels spinning wildly. For a brief moment, I felt happy. It was fleeting because my mother ran into the room, panic etched on her face, yelling at me to bring the cars back into my room. I grabbed them and ran, closing my door behind me. Disappointment crashed over me because even at that young age, I knew that feeling of freedom and happiness would not return.

I was right. When my father got home, his face contorted with anger, he pushed my bedroom door open, holding one of my little cars. In my rush to hide, I hadn't noticed I left one behind. He shouted, telling me little boys who can't clean up don't get to have nice things. All the while, he gathered every car I had and threw them away. The sight of my toys disappearing into the trash was a punch to the gut, a cruel end to my brief joy.

That was the first night I learned what leather against skin felt like. The belt whistled through the air before it bit into my flesh, the pain searing through me. I sat quietly in the corner, my body trembling, until he finally left my room. Only then did I allow the tears to fall, silent sobs shaking my small frame. They didn't stop until exhaustion claimed me and I fell asleep, my body aching, my spirit crushed.

I shake my head, bringing myself back to the present. That was the life Callum saved me from. Without him, I don't think I would've survived. He didn't even know what was going on at my house until years later, but he started inviting me to his house. Callum's home was a sanctuary, a place where laughter wasn't punished, and messes weren't met with rage. Of course, my mother was all too happy to have me gone, so it was never a fight. She saw it as one less thing to manage, one less target for my father's wrath.

Callum's friendship was a lifeline. His family welcomed me in, never questioning the frequency of my visits. In their home, I experienced a kindness and warmth that was foreign to me. It was there, in those stolen moments of peace and safety, that I began to heal, slowly piecing together the shattered fragments of my childhood.

I stayed at the Atwood house, pretending they were my real family. The kids were loud and happy. There was laughter, talking, and endless amounts of fun. The Atwood home was a symphony of joy and chaos, the complete opposite of the oppressive silence of my own home. When I was there, I felt that happiness that had been thrown in the trash, a happiness that had once seemed out of reach.

As we got older and I confided in Callum about how awful my house was, he never judged me or my shitty parents. He just listened, his face a mask of concern and understanding, never interrupting, never making me feel small for sharing my pain. He invited me over every chance he got, offering me an escape from the hell I lived in. I slept on a blowup mattress on his bedroom floor more than I slept in the bed at my house, and I loved it. That thin mattress was more comfortable than my own bed because it came with a sense of safety and belonging.

The Atwoods treated me like one of their own. Mrs. Atwood always made sure I had enough to eat, her warm smile and gentle words a stark contrast to my mother's cold indifference. Mr. Atwood would ruffle my hair and ask me about school, genuinely interested in my life. In their home, I found the family I wished I had.

So, when Callum made me promise I wouldn't date his sister, I didn't take it lightly. Callum saved me, offering me a lifeline when I was drowning in despair, and there's no way in hell I'll ever forget that. It doesn't matter how I feel about Anya, because I can't cross that line. My feelings for her are strong, but my loyalty to Callum is stronger. He's my brother in every way that counts, and betraying his trust isn't an option.

Every time I look at Anya, I remind myself of the promise I made. She's beautiful, kind, and everything I could ever want, but I owe Callum too much to risk it. The bond we share, forged in the fires of my troubled past, is something I'll never take for granted. Anya will always be a dream I can't pursue, a reminder of the sacrifices I'm willing to make for the one person who saved me from my own personal hell.

⸺

It's been almost a week since I denied Anya's kiss, and I haven't seen her once. Part of me is relieved because I still don't know what to say, but another part of me, a bigger part, misses her sweeping into the kitchen with her big smile, her energy lighting up the room. The kitchen feels emptier without her, the air heavy with the unspoken tension between us.

There's a party this weekend, and we haven't discussed the menu. I know it's because she's avoiding me, and I hate that it's now affecting our work. Our usual effortless collaboration has turned into an awkward dance of avoidance, each of us tiptoeing around the other.

"Griff, you have plans after work?" Callum asks, walking into the kitchen, breaking my train of thought.

I wipe my hands on the white towel and turn my back on the potatoes I was cutting. I lean against the counter and lift an eyebrow. "No, why?"

"My mom just called and invited us for dinner," he says, shrugging as if it's the most natural thing in the world.

"On a Wednesday?" I reply, my surprise evident in my voice.

He grabs a piece of bread off the counter and takes a bite, chewing thoughtfully before responding. "Yeah."

Atwood Sunday family dinners are a huge thing, a tradition steeped in warmth and togetherness, but Wednesday night dinners are something I've never been invited to. This unexpected invitation sends a jolt of anxiety through me. What could it mean? Is this just a casual dinner, or is there something more to it?

As I mull over the possibilities, I can't shake the feeling that this dinner might be more than just a meal. The tension between Anya and me is palpable, and I worry that her family has picked up on it. The thought of facing her tonight, in the intimacy of her family's home, fills me with a mixture of dread and anticipation.

Callum finishes his bread and looks at me expectantly, waiting for my answer. "Sure," I finally say, trying to sound casual, though my mind is racing.

"Great," he replies with a grin. "We'll head over right after work."

"This is something you guys do often?"

He shakes his head, a seriousness settling in his eyes. "No, never. I'm worried she has bad news and wants you there to help me through it."

Shit.

I nod, crossing my arms. "I'm there. What time?"

"She said around six, but I told her there's no way we could slip out that early."

"Some things are more important than work, Callum. I'll get everything prepped, and my team will be able to handle it. Tell her we'll be there."

One thing I know for sure is that life is fragile. If Carol needs us, we need to be there. To hell with everything else. The Atwood's have done so much for me; the least I can do is show up when they need me.

"You sure?" he asks, reaching for a piece of cheese from the platter on the counter.

"Yeah, buddy, I'm sure." I chuckle as he pops the cheese into his mouth. "You want me to make you something to eat?"

He grins, shaking his head. "Nah, this cheese will do for now. But thanks."

As I watch Callum, I'm reminded of the countless times he and his family have been my refuge. I can't help but think about what this dinner might mean. Could Carol have sensed the tension between Anya and me? Is this her way of addressing it, or is it simply a routine family gathering that I've been fortunate enough to be included in? The uncertainty gnaws at me, but I push it aside. Carol needs us, and that's what matters.

"I need to get back to the office and make sure everything is in order so we can leave early." He forces a grin before walking toward the door. He turns his head and says, "Thanks, Griff."

"Hey, no thanks needed."

He leaves the kitchen, and my mind wanders to what this dinner could be about. Is it a casual invitation, or is there something more behind it? The Atwood's aren't the type to hold formal interventions, but the timing and the unusual midweek gathering make me uneasy.

I push all the thoughts buzzing through my head aside and get to work preparing everything for my crew. They are perfectly capable of handling a night without me, so I'm not worried. Still, I want to ensure everything runs smoothly in my absence. I meticulously go through the prep list, double-checking every detail. From the ingredients for the weekend party to the tasks for each team member, I leave nothing to chance.

It also helps keep my mind occupied as time goes by. The rhythmic chopping of vegetables, the precise measuring of spices, and the organization of the kitchen are all distractions from the uncertainty of the evening ahead. As I work, my thoughts drift back to Anya, her smile, and the way she lights up a room. I wonder how she feels about seeing me tonight. Has she been avoiding me as deliberately as I've been avoiding her?

I set up the stations, ensuring everyone knows their responsi-bilities. My team is a well-oiled machine, each member skilled and reliable. I trust them implicitly, which makes it easier to step away, knowing they'll handle any challenge that comes their way.

"All right, guys," I call out as I gather my things. "I'm heading out for the evening. You've got everything you need, and I'm just a phone call away if anything comes up."

They nod and smile, giving me reassuring thumbs-ups and quick waves. Their confidence boosts my own, and I feel a bit more at ease as I leave the kitchen.

Callum walks into the kitchen just as I'm unbuttoning my chef's coat.

"Ready?" I ask him.

"Yeah," he says, glancing at his phone.

He hops into his car, and I climb into my truck, my stomach in knots the entire time. I'm hoping it's nothing serious, but preparing myself for the worst. I'll need to be the rock for all the Atwoods; it's the least I can do after everything they've done for me.

When we park in front of the Atwood family home, I stare at the big white house. It's always been a beacon of light in my dark life, and tonight is no different. Its welcoming presence calms me a bit, but I can't shake the anxiety gnawing at my insides.

We get out and meet on the brick walkway that leads to the front door. "It's gonna be all right, Cal," I say, slapping his back, trying to sound confident.

"Yeah," he mutters, but his voice lacks conviction.

The front door opens before we even reach it, and Carol stands there with a huge smile on her face. "I'm so glad you could both make it," she says warmly.

Callum doesn't say anything, just wraps her in a tight hug. I need to look away so my emotions don't get the better of me. Seeing their bond always tugs at my heartstrings, reminding me of what I missed out on growing up.

"Callum, what's wrong, son?" Carol asks, her smile fading into a look of concern as she holds him.

I step inside behind them and see the worry on her face. "We're here now, Mom. Just tell us," Callum says, his voice steady but with an edge of urgency.

Her brows furrow as she looks between us, confusion evident. "Tell you what?"

"Carol, we're here for you," I add, my voice gentle yet firm, trying to convey that we're ready for whatever news she has.

She looks puzzled for a moment, then laughs softly. "Oh, boys, there's nothing wrong. You two are always so thoughtful. I invited you to dinner because Tripp is out and your father and I are going out for a fancy dinner, and I didn't want Anya eating alone."

Callum steps back, crossing his muscular arms over his chest. "You're kidding, right? You didn't actually pull us away from work because you want us to babysit?"

She hits him lightly with the kitchen towel she's holding as she smiles. "Your sister doesn't need to be babysat, silly boy. She needs company. She's been a little down." Her soft eyes slide to mine, and I feel myself stiffen. "I think she just needs a friend."

My heart cracks in my chest, knowing I'm the reason she's feeling this way. The guilt weighs heavily on me, each glance from Carol a reminder of the turmoil I've caused.

"Mom, what the hell? There's nothing wrong with you? You aren't dying? No one is dying?" Callum yells, his voice echoing through the hallway.

It sounds muffled to me, though, as I keep thinking of Anya. The image of her smile haunts me, a stark contrast to the sadness Carol hinted at.

"Callum Atwood, don't raise your voice to me," Carol scolds, her tone firm. "You need to realize what an asset your sister is to that brewery. She needs to hear it. So stop being such a hardhead and do what you know is right." She shakes her head and looks at me. "Griffin, you're here to keep them from going at each other's throats."

"Mom..." Callum starts, but she holds up her hand as Don walks down the stairs.

"Dinner is ready. It's staying warm in the oven. Anya is in the shower, so it would be nice if you had everything set for her when she gets out." She tosses her apron at Callum and smiles. "Have fun."

A night with Anya and Callum. This really is bad news.

Callum catches the apron, grumbling under his breath as he heads to the kitchen. I follow, trying to shake off the unease that's settled in my gut. The kitchen is warm and inviting, the smell of lasagne and fresh bread filling the air. Callum starts pulling dishes from the oven, and I set the table, my movements automatic as my mind races.

"Dude, can you believe this?" Callum mutters, placing a few dishes on the counter. "All this fuss just because Anya's feeling a bit down?"

"She's your sister, Callum. Sometimes it's the little things that matter," I reply, trying to sound nonchalant. But inside, I'm a mess. I know I'm the reason she's feeling down, and it tears me apart.

We set everything up, and I can hear the faint sound of the shower running upstairs. My thoughts keep drifting to Anya, wondering how she'll react when she sees me. Will she be angry? Sad? Indifferent? The uncertainty is killing me.

Chapter 9

Anya

I hear voices when I step out of the shower, but I figure it's just my mom and dad. My mother's been excited about making lasagna, and she even told me she made something special for dessert. I don't know why she's going all out on dinner, but whatever. It's a comforting thought, considering the turmoil inside me.

My phone dings on my dresser, and I pick it up, checking the text that just came through.

> Willow: Sex is highly overrated, right? Like there's no reason I should expect too much from Lake, right?

I stare at the text thread between Willow, Hartford, and me.

Hartford: Sex is never overrated. When you're with the right man it's worth it.

Willow: How do you know if you're with the right man? I care a lot about Lake, but we just can't seem to get the sex right.

Is it that bad?

Willow: Maybe there's something wrong with me. Maybe I'm just not a sexual person.

I can totally relate. I think sex is overrated. That mind-numbing sex they talk about in romance novels isn't real.

Hartford: I beg to differ. Sex between Pax and me is off the charts. (Sorry Anya)

I laugh, and am grossed out at the exact same time, but it makes me wonder if Hartford is right. Is there life-changing sex out there?

Willow: It's not just the sex between Lake and me that's bad. We've been sort of fighting a lot.

Hartford: About what?

Willow: I don't even know, tbh. He's always sort of controlling.

Dump him. You don't need that in your life.

Hartford: Controlling in the bedroom is a plus, but not in ordinary life. Do you even see a future with him?

Willow: Not really. It was just nice having somebody. I don't want to be alone forever. And he's not controlling in the bedroom. He's not really anything in the bedroom.

You won't be.

I put my phone down, thinking about my own life. Will I be alone forever? My head's been a mess since I put it all out there on the line with Griffin. How had I read the signals wrong? I replay our interactions over and over, trying to pinpoint where I misunderstood his intentions. The confusion and disappointment are like a weight on my chest. Whatever the case, I read them *so* wrong.

I finish towel drying my hair, tossing on a pair of jeans and a cute red top that hangs off both shoulders. The color is vibrant, a stark contrast to my mood. I don't bother putting on makeup because it's just a normal night at home. The natural look seems fitting for how exposed I feel after everything with Griffin. I have to work this weekend, and after dinner, I plan on getting a hold of Griffin to discuss the menu. Despite everything, work must go on, and I need to maintain some sense of normalcy.

As I head downstairs, the voices become clearer, and I realize there are more people here than just my parents. I step into the dining room and see Griffin and Callum setting the table. My heart skips a beat, and I freeze at the doorway, momentarily taken aback.

"Hey, Anya," Griffin says, his voice sounding more confident than I feel.

"Griff? What are you doing here?" I ask, trying to keep my tone neutral, though I'm sure the surprise is evident on my face.

Callum snaps his eyes to mine. "Mom and Dad went out. They asked Griff and I to babysit you."

I park a hand on my hip as I slowly slide my eyes to meet Griffin's. "Is that true?"

How embarrassing.

"She didn't ask us to babysit. She's just worried about you." Griffin's kind eyes slay me, and it makes me relive the moment he denied me play out again in my mind.

"She thinks you're depressed," Callum says, with his usual sneer. "Are you blue?"

"Shut up." I'm going to let my mother have it when she gets home. How could she call them? "Well, I'm not sad, so you two can go home." I try to shoo them out of the dining room, but Callum stands still.

"I'm fucking starving. I'm not going anywhere." Callum sits at the head of the table, and Griffin and I take a seat on either side of him, across from one another.

I can't even look at him.

"Hey," Griffin says, holding the salad bowl in his hands. "Do you want salad?"

I snatch the bowl from him. "Thank you," I say reluctantly.

"When are we doing this horse thing?" Callum asks after swallowing his bite of lasagne.

"We don't have to go." I finish plating my salad, and grab a roll from the basket. "It was a stupid idea."

Griffin takes the bowl from my outstretched hand, and his finger grazes across my pinky. And it's like lightning strikes. "No, I think it's a great idea. We're excited about going," he looks at Callum. "Right, Cal?"

Callum shrugs. "I guess. Sure, why the fuck not."

I can't understand why Griffin's trying to make me feel better. Ugh, it's because he denied me and now he doesn't want to hurt my feelings. Just like a big brother would do.

My appetite disintegrates, and I scrape my chair across the hardwood as I stand. "I'm going for a walk." I leave the house in a flash, not even sure where I'm going, but I need to get there fast.

My feet move to their own volition, bringing me further and further away from the house.

"Anya, wait," I hear Griffin's voice call out behind me.

I spin around, crossing my arms over my chest. "You don't need to look out after me. I'm not your little sister."

His face twists as he blinks at me. "I definitely don't think of you like a little sister."

"You hurt my feelings," I admit, and then inwardly cringe at how pathetic I sound.

"I'm sorry," he says, and I feel the pain subside.

There's just something about him. Griffin has a way of setting my soul free. Like his words make me feel all warm and bubbly inside. It's weird.

I need to head back into the house before Callum comes out to investigate.

"So," I say a bit awkwardly. "Horseback riding. Are you up for it?"

Griffin smiles and it nearly takes my breath away. "I can't wait."

What was I thinking when I agreed to take Callum and Griffin horseback riding? The sun sits high in the sky, casting a warm, golden glow over everything. The weather is absolutely perfect —better than any day I've ever experienced. The temperature is just right, not too hot and definitely not cold. A gentle breeze rustles the leaves, adding to the idyllic atmosphere.

However, there's one significant problem. Callum is nowhere to be found.

"I just tried his cell phone, and nothing," Griffin says, sliding his phone into the back pocket of his jeans. He looks good today, I notice. His dark jeans fit him perfectly, and his white t-shirt with the phrase '*Chop It Like It's Hot*' printed across the chest adds a touch of humor to his casual look. His hair is slightly tousled, and there's a relaxed confidence about him that makes him seem effortlessly stylish.

I can't help but feel a mix of irritation and worry. Where could Callum be? He was so excited about this outing, and now he's MIA. The stable owner is giving us curious looks, probably wondering if we're going to cancel. The horses are ready, their coats gleaming in the sunlight, and I can feel the anticipation in the air.

Griffin's brow furrows slightly, and I can tell he's concerned too. "Maybe he's just running late," he suggests, trying to sound optimistic. But there's a hint of doubt in his voice.

We stand there in the paddock, the smell of hay and leather mixing with the fresh scent of the outdoors. The other riders are mounting up, and I feel a pang of envy. This was supposed to be a fun, carefree day. I glance around, hoping to catch sight of Callum sprinting towards us, but there's nothing. Just the serene landscape and the occasional chirp of a bird.

"Should we wait a bit longer or start without him?" I ask, feeling the weight of the decision pressing down on me. Griffin checks his watch, his expression thoughtful.

It isn't the first time Callum has bailed on an outing.

Griffin grabs his phone once more. "I'm calling the restaurant," he says, punching at his phone.

"Don't bother. Even if he is there, by the time he makes it here..." my words fall away thinking about my brother and how he's most likely at work. I swear he doesn't know how to have fun. "We can just ride ourselves," I tell Griffin.

Mr. Daniels smiles at us. "So, just the two of ya, then?"

I nod. "I'm so sorry about this. You know Callum," I say with a shrug.

Mr. Daniels laughs, because he does in fact know Callum very well. We used to play on this ranch when we were kids. Mr. Daniels taught us all how to ride, even Griffin. So, we're not new to horses.

"Just take them down to the watering hole, and let them rest and drink, and then you can bring them back later this afternoon." Mr. Daniels tips his hat at us as he walks the third horse back.

I grab the reins of Silver, my favorite horse. It's been a while since I've ridden. Silver's a beautiful Quarab horse with a coat of black and white hairs, giving it an almost silver appearance. Silver is the most intelligent horse I've ever known, and I'm happy I get to be the one riding her.

I mount Silver, and once I'm steady in the saddle, I walk her over to where Griffin stands in front of the American Paint horse, Honey, he'll be riding.

He mounts Honey, and then we're off, both of our horses moving side-by-side together. The wind in my hair reminds me why I love riding so much.

We move like fire through the fields, eating up the distance with ease. Silver runs smooth, and it's like no time has passed as she remembers me. I see the watering hole coming up fast, and I pull on the reins to slow Silver down.

Once we reach a good stopping point, I start to dismount. My foot gets snagged, and oh my god, I go down.

Fast.

Hard.

Oww.

My foot slips in something wet, and I land flat on my back. "What the…" my question slips out as I feel something slick down my back.

Griffin's eyes are horrified as he moves quickly to dismount and rush over to where I'm still lying in the grass. He makes quick work of securing the horses, and he reaches out his hand.

"I think I landed in poo," I tell him, wondering how my horse could have taken a dump so quickly before I even got off his back.

"I think you slipped in it too."

I take his hand, and he helps me up. "Umm," I say, trying to look at my ass to see how bad it is. "I feel it all over my arms."

Griffin laughs as he looks at me. "You have it everywhere. It's in your hair." He points to my hair. "Get in the water."

"What?" I ask him, looking mortified. This is the worst thing that could possibly happen to me. It's bad enough I'm covered in poo, but to have Griffin here makes it ten times worse. "Your clothes look spared, just a bit on your shirt. Maybe a bit around your ankle on your jeans." He cracks a smile. "But your hair and face."

I swat my hand along my forehead. "My face?" I question, smearing more of the shit all over me.

Griffin laughs harder. "I don't mean to laugh," he says. "But it's all over you."

My hand is covered, and I take it and run it over Griffin's arm.

He stops laughing instantly. "You did not just do that." He stares at his arm like it's got the plague.

Now I'm smiling, backing away from him. "Don't hurt me," I say, rushing away from him.

He chases after me. "Anya, oh I'm definitely getting you back for this."

I hold up my hands. "Don't get any closer," I say, using my poo-covered hands as weapons.

"You're disgusting," he says through a laugh.

I glance over at the watering hole. There's really only one thing left to do. "Turn around," I tell him.

He stares at me, obviously confused. "Why?"

"Because I'm going to take off my clothes and get in the water. You should wash your arm off too."

Griffin's eyes darken as he studies me. I probably look disgusting with horse poop all over me, but he doesn't stare at me like I am. "All of your clothes?"

"I'll leave my underwear and bra on. Just like a bikini," I say, parking a hand on my hip. "Are you going to turn around, or do I have to get undressed in front of you," I challenge him.

He spins around so fast, ripping his shirt off. "I'll wash my arm off," he says, moving closer to the water.

I unzip my jeans, and fling my shirt off, trying my best not to get them dirtier than they already are. I can't believe this is happening.

I'm in nothing but my hot pink bra and panties, and I move closer to the water, hoping Griffin doesn't turn around.

But kind of wanting him to.

Chapter 10

Griffin

My arm has horse shit on it. I should be gagging, but instead, I'm on my knees washing it in the lake trying to keep myself distracted from looking at a nearly naked Anya.

When she first fell off the horse, my heart sank, thinking she hurt herself. As I rushed over, it took all my willpower not to burst out laughing when I saw her lying in a pile of horse shit. But now that I know she's undressing behind me, it's not so funny.

The urge to turn around has me physically shaking. Being around her all day has been difficult enough. Ever since she put herself out there, it's hard for me to concentrate on anything else. I replay that night in my head constantly and each time it ends with me claiming her full lips. Now, she just steps away from me, wet, in nothing but her bra and panties.

I deserve a fucking medal for keeping my distance.

"Griffin."

Shit, I can't ignore her, but if I turn around my promise to Callum will be shot to hell.

"Griffin?"

Fuck.

I stand up, still keeping my back to her and wipe my wet arm with my hand. "What's up?"

"I need your help."

I squeeze my eyes shut, trying to block out images of what I'd like to help her with. Like slamming my lips to hers while I pull her wet body against mine or helping her out of the thin material she has left on.

I haven't looked at her and I know without a doubt that she looks sexy as hell. It's killing me trying to do the right thing. Physically and mentally.

If I hadn't made that damn promise I would've kissed her and I'd be in the water with her right now and she'd be asking for my help to give her the relief she's desperate to get.

"Nevermind," she mumbles.

Christ. I scrub my face and turn around. Worst mistake of my life.

Anya is in the water, which is not doing a good job of covering her. I can see her hard nipples poking out of her bright-pink bra. Her long hair is dripping wet, causing drops of water to roll down her gorgeous face.

She takes my breath away.

I clear my throat as I try to keep my eyes on hers instead of her incredibly sexy body. "What do you need?"

Please, say me.

"It's fine. I was just going to ask if I got it all," she says, glancing down at herself.

Now because I took so long to acknowledge her, she thinks I didn't want to see her. Which is the complete opposite of what I'm feeling.

I let my eyes roam over her and the look of hurt is back on her beautiful face. Frustrated, I kick off my sneakers and unbuckle my jeans, making a pile with my now discarded clothes.

I walk toward the water and her moss-green eyes widen. "What are you doing?"

I wish I could tell her the need I have to be close to her right now is undeniable, but I don't. Instead I grin as I step into the water. "I'm making sure you're poop free before you get out."

That medal I said I should receive, is now sinking to the bottom of this lake as my dick moves higher.

I should stop eye-fucking her, but if I'm honest, she's doing the same to me. I can feel her gaze burning into my flesh as she takes in every inch of me. It's turning me on more, which I didn't think was possible.

She laughs, shaking her head as I get closer. "I didn't mean you should get in the lake."

I reach her and our eyes lock. "I know you didn't, Anya," I whisper, moving a piece of wet hair off her cheek.

My eyes bounce between hers and her breathing picks up, matching my own. She blushes and it's incredibly sexy seeing the effect on her. I allow my eyes to drag over her, making sure she's clean, but slightly taking advantage of the situation as I burn her near naked body to memory.

"You look good, Anya." My eyes move back to hers and I can see the lust there. "Real fucking good," I whisper.

She visibly swallows and I should fight it harder. I should walk out of this lake and just allow things to stay the way they are. I shouldn't push the limits or cross any lines.

"Fuck this," I growl, sinking my fingers into her wet hair and pressing my lips to hers.

Her full lips are soft as silk against mine. I run my tongue against the seam of her mouth and she gives me the access I'm seeking. Our tongues touch and it's electric.

I deepen the kiss as I tighten my hold in her hair and she lets out a soft moan that sends a shot straight to my dick. My hands trail down her back and into the water, resting on her round ass. I push my hard cock against her and we both moan at the connection.

I've fantasized about kissing her since I rejected her and in every one of those fantasies, it was never this good. Not even remotely close.

Her skin against mine feels like silk. Her hard nipples rubbing on my bare chest is making my dick incredibly hard. The way her tongue dances with mine is like a promise for more.

My fingers sink into her ass as we both get lost in this explosive kiss. Her hands move up and down my back, searing my skin even in this cool water.

I won't be able to walk away from her after this. I can't.

I've never felt what I feel right now.

Never more turned on.

Never more connected.

Never more alive.

Fuck, what is she doing to me?

Just as I think it, I feel her hands on my shoulders and she pushes away from me. Her eyes wide as she reaches up, touching her swollen lips.

She shakes her head, backing away from me. "You're just doing this because you feel guilty."

"Anya."

"No, no, I don't want your pity kiss."

I move toward her, grabbing lightly onto her arm to stop her from moving further away. "Anya, I don't give out pity kisses. I don't let guilt blindly lead me into something I'll regret." I move my hands into her hair and search her green eyes. "I didn't kiss you because you tried kissing me. I kissed you because I needed it. I didn't just want it, I needed it. That was as real as it gets, don't ever question that."

I can hear my phone ringing, but I ignore it, keeping my focus on her.

"Your phone is ringing," she says.

"You're more important."

She tilts her head slightly as her eyes soften. "Griffin," she breathes out.

My phone rings again and we both look over at it.

"Go," she insists.

"No." I shake my head. "I'm not walking away this time while you question what happened."

My phone rings again and now I know it's something important. No one would call this many times if it wasn't. I search her eyes, hoping she'll say she knows this was real, hoping she'll say anything, because rushing out of this water without her understanding will kill me.

"You felt how turned on I was. How could you question that?"

She blows out a breath. "I know." She nods and grabs my upper arm. "I know, Griffin."

I grin, but before I can say anything, my phone is ringing again.

"Fuck."

We both rush out of the water toward my jeans and I grab my phone out of my pocket, and I answer it.

"Griffin?" a voice I recognize says.

My eyes slide to Anya as I say, "Tripp?"

"What's wrong?" she whispers.

I shrug, focusing back on the call. "Something wrong?"

"Listen, I need help and I can't call my parents or any of my brothers. I'm at the police station and I need someone to pick me up," he says.

My eyes widen as I snap my head to Anya. "The police station. What the fuck did you do, Tripp?"

Anya rushes over grabbing her clothes, so I begin pulling mine on too. We're both wet, but we have no choice.

"Please, Griff. My family can't find out. I'm begging for your help here."

"It's gonna be a little bit, but I'll get there as fast as I can."

I hang up and pocket my phone, walking over to Anya.

She pulls her shirt on as I step next to her. "What did he do?"

"I don't know, he didn't say. He doesn't want any of you to know," I say.

She gives a humorless laugh and climbs back up onto Silver. "Too bad. Let's go get him."

I climb back onto Honey and we begin the trek back to the ranch. "Anya, are we going to talk about what happened?"

Her eyes slide to mine and she raises an eyebrow. "I think getting my little brother out of the slammer is more important."

Anger I have no right to feel, burns through me. I just risked everything putting myself out there to her and she acts like it was nothing.

"I'll meet you at the car," she says, her horse taking off in a quick gallop.

I trot Honey and he takes off, kicking up dust behind him.

Fucking Tripp ruining the moment.

Fucking Callum and his promise.

Fucking Atwoods are killing me.

Chapter 11

Anya

Once I settle into the front seat of Griffin's truck, I lean back in the seat, looking out the window. I wonder what Tripp is doing getting in trouble with the police.

Sure, he's been hanging out with the wrong crowd, and coming home late at night, but I figured it was like every eighteen-year-old who isn't serious about anything in life.

"I'll bring you back for your car later," Griffin says as he pulls onto the road to lead us back to town.

"Thank you," I whisper. I know Griffin wants to talk about what happened in the lake, but I can't bring myself to even think about it. "You're a fixer," I say, barely audible.

"What?" he asks.

I turn to face him. "You're a fixer. You always have been." I don't know much about Griffin's life, but I do know how he's always been the one to fix things when we were younger.

"What's that supposed to mean?"

"You've always been the one to fix things. Look at my brothers, every time they fight you're the voice of reason to calm them all down, fixing the issues between them. Remember when Millie opened her bookstore? You were the one to gather everyone in town to help her fix the place up."

"Everyone but Tripp showed up," Griffin says, remembering back to that sunny afternoon.

I laugh lightly, remembering what Tripp said. "Tripp said he'd get hives being around that many books."

Griffin laughs. "So, I fix things, that doesn't mean I didn't want to kiss you."

My chest gets all warm and fuzzy, but I try to keep my wits about me. "It kind of does. You knew I was upset about trying to kiss you, and you wanted to fix it. It's fine. We shouldn't be kissing anyways because we work together," I say, knowing that nothing good can come from kissing Griffin.

It's not like he'd ever want to date me.

Griffin doesn't say anything to what I said, and I guess it's better that way. I look out the window again, watching the passing greenery blur before me. My thoughts turn to Tripp, and I worry my bottom lip between my teeth.

Griffin's hand lands on my thigh, and it sends a jolt of electricity traveling up my spine. "I'm sure he'll be okay."

"I feel like he's never going to grow up. Like he has some sort of death wish or something."

Griffin removes his hand, and I instantly miss the warmth of it. "He's just taking longer to grow up than the rest of us."

"It's because my mother spoils him," I say with a smile, and I think about Griffin. I don't know much about his home life growing up. Except that he was at our house more than his own. "What about you?" I ask him.

"What about me?"

"Did your mother spoil you?"

Griffin's dark eyes meet mine quickly before he focuses back on the road. But in that moment I see a lifetime of pain hidden behind his irises. It makes me regret my question.

"You don't have to tell me," I say, wishing I could erase this quiet moment stretching between us.

"How much of my life has Callum told you?"

"He's told me nothing. In case you haven't noticed, Callum and I aren't what you'd call close."

Griffin blows out a deep breath. "Growing up wasn't easy in my house. My mother tried, but she cared more about keeping my father happy than about me."

"I'm so sorry. I didn't know."

Griffin's hand lands back on my thigh, and I reach down and rest my hand over his, hoping he'll continue telling me about his life. "My father was an asshole. Well, he still is. I haven't seen him in years and that's how I like it."

"I think I've maybe seen your dad once in my whole life."

Griffin's father toils away at the lumber yard situated on the outskirts of our small town, his presence casting a shadow over our community. Despite the lack of formal introductions, his reputation precedes him. "Yeah, you're fortunate not to cross paths with him. He's not the most pleasant person," Griffin confides in me.

"I'm sorry," I respond, feeling a pang of empathy for Griffin. "It makes sense now why you spent so much time at our place."

"Callum never questioned it. He just welcomed me in whenever he could," Griffin shares, a hint of gratitude coloring his voice.

I can't help but smile. "It's reassuring to know that Cal does have a heart. I was beginning to wonder."

Griffin chuckles softly, the warmth of his touch seeping through my jeans as his thumb draws gentle circles. "I honestly can't fathom where I'd be without Callum. Probably six feet under or behind bars. That's why I'd go to the ends of the earth for your family."

His tender gesture leaves me feeling light-headed, prompting me to shift my fingers to trace the contours of his hand. "I'm grateful he was able to be that support for you. Have you spoken to your parents recently?"

Griffin removes his hand, placing it back on the wheel so he can make a turn toward the police station. "Last time I talked to them was before I left for culinary school. My father told me I was being an ungrateful piece of shit leaving like I was, and that I needed to get a job and help out with the bills around the house." Griffin swings into the parking lot, pulling his truck into a spot. He kills the ignition, and turns to face me. "I felt bad for leaving. For a long time I felt I should have helped my parents pay bills, but I felt I could help them more if I made something of myself." He hangs his head low. "I don't know," he blows out.

I want to hug him. Something inside me explodes with emotion as I sit here and stare at him. He's really quite gorgeous, but it's more than that. There's this vulnerability there that makes me want to reach out and touch him in some way. "I'm glad you left," I tell him, happy he went to make something of himself. "You love cooking."

His eyes crash into mine. "I do love it."

My heart squeezes in my chest, having his full attention on me. It makes me want to lean in and kiss him again, but I know that's not the answer.

This man has done everything he can for our family. He feels like he owes us in some small way, and I'm sure that's why he felt he needed to make things right with me.

I can't lay that on him.

I shouldn't have tried to come onto him. I'm an asshole.

"You're a good man," I tell him, because it's true.

Something flickers behind his eyes as he stares at me. "Let's go and get your brother."

"Will you do one thing for me?" I ask him.

"Sure. You know I'd do anything for you."

I smile, my heart doing that flippity-flop thing it always seems to do in Griffin's presence. "Please keep me from killing him."

Chapter 12

Griffin

I grin, squeezing her hand at her request, knowing she's joking but I almost feel the same. What the hell is Tripp thinking? "I'll do my best."

We climb out of the truck and make our way into the police station. I hold the door open for Anya and the bright lights hit us as soon as we enter.

"My stomach is in knots and I haven't done anything, but walking in the police station makes me feel like I'm in trouble for something," she whispers.

I grab her hand and squeeze, letting her know I'm right here. "You've done nothing wrong."

I'm not even sure if I'm trying to convince her or myself. That kiss has my head all messed up. Not because it wasn't amazing, but because it *was* amazing and she doesn't appear to see it like I do. At this point, I don't know if I keep trying to prove

I wanted the kiss or if I just let it go and remember the promise I made to Callum.

"Griffin, Anya."

We turn and Sheriff Brown is standing there with his big arms crossed. I haven't seen this man in a hot minute.

"Sheriff, it's great to see you. Wish it was under different circumstances. What happened?" I ask.

"It's great to see you two," he says, grinning as his eyes bounce between us. We're still holding hands and this looks like much more than what it really is. He clears his throat as he shakes his head, his bushy eyebrows raising as he stares at us. "We got a call about a party at an abandoned house. When we arrived, everyone ran, but Tripp was too drunk to make it out as fast as everyone else."

"During the day?" Anya questions.

"Yeah, apparently they've been there since last night partying."

"So, what happens now?" I ask.

"I should keep him until he's sober, but as I told him, he's lucky I've known him since he was in diapers. I allowed him to make a phone call." He chuckles, adjusting his heavy belt. "I shouldn't be surprised he called you instead of his parents, or brothers."

"Yeah, he thinks calling me will keep him out of trouble, but I'll make sure he's punished in my own way."

He nods. "The crew he was hanging out with are known to us. He's going to end up getting himself in real trouble if he keeps hanging out with them."

"This is unbelievable. He knows better," Anya says, shaking her head, clearly upset.

"He's young and dumb. Hopefully, this has scared him enough to see things differently," I say, hoping to ease her concerns.

"Let's hope so," Sheriff Brown says.

"What do we do now?" Anya asks.

"We aren't hitting him with any charges, this time. So, you guys are free to take him home. I'll go back and get him out of the holding cell."

"Thanks," she whispers.

"I'll take him to my place tonight so he can sober up," I say, staring at the door Sheriff Brown just entered.

"What the hell is wrong with him? Doesn't he realize how fortunate he is? When he finishes high school he doesn't even need to bust his ass in college because his future is set at the brewery. He's being selfish."

"I know it feels that way, but that's not how he sees it. He's young and he's trying to find out who he is. He might not be trying to escape a bad situation, but he's trying to escape something," I explain.

I did everything I could to escape my home life at Tripp's age. Even spent a few nights here and there in an abandoned house when the Atwood's were out of town. I'm not sure what Tripp is trying to escape from because his family life couldn't be more perfect. But there's something going on and I'm going to find out what it is.

"What could he be trying to escape?" Anya asks with a shaky voice.

The need to wrap her into my arms overpowers me, and I stuff my hands into my pockets so I won't touch her. Even though I'm slowly dying inside.

"Maybe he had his heart broken."

It's not a bad guess. Heartbreak does make people do crazy things.

Her eyes bounce between mine as she visibly swallows. "Have you ever had your heart broken?"

The need overwhelms me and I reach out, touching her cheek, but before I can say anything, the heavy door slams, causing her to jump.

"Tripp Nolan Atwood," Anya says, moving toward him with a raised finger pointing at him.

Tripp's eyes snap to mine and narrow. "Thanks for keeping this between us."

"Oh no, you don't get to be pissed at anyone when we're here picking you up from jail," Anya hisses.

"Anya, it's not a big deal," he says, shoving his hands into his pockets with a shrug of his shoulder.

She gives a humorless laugh, pinning him with her angry gaze. "Not a big deal? Really? How about I have Sheriff Brown put your ungrateful ass back in the cell with all the other criminals? You can take a piss with everyone staring at you."

Sheriff Brown lightly chuckles beside me and I slap his back. "Sheriff, can we keep this between us? I'd rather not get the Atwoods involved. I'll handle Tripp."

His brown eyes lift to mine and he nods. "I won't say anything, but I'm not sure your girlfriend will be able to keep the same promise."

"Oh, she's not my girlfriend."

"Really? It sure looked that way."

My heart squeezes as I look back at Anya as she yells at Tripp. "Yeah, we're just friends," I whisper.

"Griffin, you're a good man. Don't let the past interfere with that fact." Before I can say anything, he walks over to Tripp and grabs his shoulder. "I don't want to see you in here again. You understand me?" His voice is foreboding. Authoritative. Scary as fuck.

"Yes, sir," Tripp says.

"You won't see him again. If you do, you have my permission to use your nightstick," Anya rushes out.

"Am I free to go?" Tripp asks.

"Yes," Sheriff Brown says.

Tripp keeps his eyes locked on mine as he moves toward me. He knocks into my shoulder as he passes and I clench my fists.

Time to get him alone.

"Come on, Anya." She storms after him and I run my hand through my hair. "Thanks again, Sheriff."

"Good luck with both of them. You know how stubborn the Atwoods can be," he says, chuckling as he walks away.

When I get outside, Anya and Tripp are yelling at each other by my truck.

"You're out of control, Tripp. Get your shit together."

"Shut the fuck up," he yells at her.

I rush over and slam him against the truck, getting right in his face. "Don't ever talk to your sister like that again. You want to be a disrespectful little shit I'll leave you right here while I call your parents."

"Get off me," he growls, pushing at me but making zero progress.

"If I ever hear you talk to her like that again, I promise you will regret it," I hiss, pushing off of him.

He straightens his shirt as I unlock the door. We all climb in and when I start the truck Tripp leans his body on the center console and looks between us. "So, are you two dating or something?"

"No, of course not," Anya rushes out.

It shouldn't hurt like it does, because we aren't dating, but the way she rushed it out feels like I'm a toxic plague.

"So that show of force was for no reason?" he pushes.

I reach over and shove him back into his seat. "That show of force was me reminding you to respect your sister and all women. You never speak to them like that. It's disgusting behavior and makes you look like an asshole."

The number of times I wanted to pin my father against a wall for speaking to my mother like that is countless. Hearing Tripp speak to Anya like that brought my past into my present and I couldn't help myself. I'll be damned if I'm going to allow someone who's like a brother to me, act like that man.

"I'm sorry, Anya," he whispers.

"You need to sober up and get your shit together," she says, crossing her arms.

Even though Tripp has questioned this situation, it doesn't stop me from reaching over and resting my hand on her knee.

I can feel her eyes on me as I drive toward the ranch and I grin. "I've got this."

I keep my hand on her until we pull up next to her car. This isn't how I saw this night ending, but life is constantly throwing curve balls that you need to handle.

Anya turns in her seat and looks back at Tripp. "I don't know what is going on with you, Tripp, but I really hope you get it straightened out because I know this isn't the man you are."

With that she opens the door and climbs out of the truck. I rush out to meet her, grabbing her hand before she can open her car door.

"Anya, I'm going to talk to him. Please don't let it consume you."

She smiles and pushes up on her toes, pressing a soft kiss to my cheek. "See, you're the fixer."

I want to push her against the car and slam my lips to hers. I want to pick up where we left off in the water. I want to feel her body against mine again and hear the sounds of pleasure that escape her.

But I don't. I simply nod and step back.

I know she feels what I feel, but she's fighting it.

The question is, do I pursue the forbidden or do I let her go before I even have her?

"Thank you, Griffin."

She climbs into her car and I watch her drive off. I glance back at my truck and narrow my eyes. Time to deal with the little jailbird.

The drive to my place is quiet, but when I pull into the driveway, he leans forward. "Why are we at your place?"

"Oh I'm sorry, did you want me to drop you off drunk to your parents and have them question where I picked you up from?" He drops back into the seat and I open my door. "That's what I thought. Let's go."

He follows me inside and falls onto the couch. "I can't believe you brought Anya."

I sit next to him, handing him a bottle of water. "I can't believe you were arrested. I think instead of being pissed your sister knows, you should tell me what the hell is going on with you."

He shakes his head, staring at the dark TV in front of us. "I was out with friends. Why do you assume it means something is going on? I was looking for some fun. Looking for some pussy."

"Watch your damn mouth," I hiss.

"Stop acting like you're better than me, Griff. I hear the way you and my brothers talk and tease each other. Pussy is not the worst thing I could say."

He's not wrong.

"That group you were with, do you hang out with them a lot?"

"Why?"

There's my answer.

"They're trouble, Tripp. Why the hell do you want to get mixed up with that crowd?"

"They are fun and people judge them for having fun."

"They all ran and let you take the fall tonight. None of them came looking for you at the police station. I bet none of them have even texted to check if you're good. These aren't the people you used to hang out with. What happened to those guys?"

He sighs and rests his head against the back of the couch. "I fucked up tonight, I get it. But there's no deep meaning here, Griff. Just let it go."

"There are other ways to escape things, Tripp. Alcohol and the wrong crowd aren't the way. I had to escape shit and I can help you, but you need to fucking be honest with me."

He turns his head and looks at me. For a minute I can see I've gotten through to him, but it disappears quickly. "Not escaping anything, Griff. Please let me get some sleep. I feel like shit."

I laugh and stand up. "You sleep tonight, little man, because tomorrow you're going to wish you had the alcohol blocking out what I'm saying. This little jail pick up is not a favor. You'll be working it off. Long nights with me by your side. You'll be so tired of looking at my face that you'll wish you called someone else." I go to the bathroom closet and grab some extra blankets and a pillow, tossing them on him. "Sleep well."

When I get into bed I think of the look on Tripp's face. Something is bothering him and I'm determined to figure it out.

My phone vibrates on the nightstand and I pick it up.

Anya: Just checking in.

He's ready to serve his sentence with Warden Cole starting tomorrow.

Anya: LOL good! Don't go easy on him.

I told you I've got this, don't worry.

Anya: It's hard not to worry when we picked up my little brother from the police station.

I know, but you aren't alone. We'll do this together.

Anya: Thank you, Griffin.

Always.

Anya: I can't stop thinking about that kiss.

Fuck. I close my eyes, relieved and turned on. My body hardens at the thought.

Me either. Come over for dinner Monday night. Let's talk.

Anya: Okay.

She agreed. I'm not pressing my luck. I put my phone down and smile.

I guess I'm going to pursue the forbidden.

Chapter 13

Anya

When you love somebody and you see them hurting, it pains you deeply, igniting a fierce desire to do whatever it takes to ease their suffering and bring them peace.

Something's going on with Tripp. Something I don't fully understand, but I want to help make it better. I could very easily walk downstairs and talk to my mother. Ask her what she thinks it could be, but I don't want to betray his trust. For I fear that would only make things worse. I could ask one of the many brothers I have, but again, if Tripp hasn't confided in any of them, I know I shouldn't either.

The only person he trusted to turn to was Griffin.

That speaks volumes.

Griffin is more a part of this family than I ever really thought.

As I sit in my room, going over the specifics for the party on Friday night, I can't help but think about Griffin asking me to dinner. What does he need to talk to me about? My mind races through possibilities, but I'm guessing it has to do with how we're going to help Tripp. I haven't seen Griffin or Tripp since the other day when we picked Tripp up from the police station. The memory of that tense evening still lingers in my mind.

I push my notebook away and rummage through my closet, searching for the perfect outfit. What should I wear? I try on dress after dress, discarding each one after scrutinizing my reflection. The butterflies in my stomach intensify with each discarded outfit.

Finally, I spot a dress I haven't worn in a while. It's a deep emerald green, a color that always makes my eyes pop. The fabric is soft and flows elegantly, hugging my curves in all the right places. I slip it on and step in front of the mirror. The dress features a sweetheart neckline and delicate lace sleeves, adding a touch of sophistication. The skirt flares out just enough to give it a playful swing, but not so much that it feels too formal.

I pair the dress with a simple silver necklace and matching earrings, completing the look with a pair of strappy black heels. As I take one last look in the mirror, I feel a surge of confidence. This dress is perfect. It's elegant yet understated, striking the right balance for a dinner that promises to be significant.

With my outfit decided, I take a deep breath and prepare myself for whatever conversation lies ahead with Griffin.

I pull up to his house right at seven, and turn off the ignition. His house is warm and friendly, and it gives me a sense of pride with how well Griffin has done for himself. I've never met his parents, but from what he said, they don't sound like nice people.

I exit the car, walk up his front porch, and ring the bell. Nerves flutter low in my belly as I wait for him to answer the door.

"Hey," he says, appearing in the doorway like a knight in shining armor. "The door was open, you could have just walked in." He steps aside so I can enter his home.

I push a strand of my hair behind my ear as I step over the threshold. "I didn't want to be rude."

Griffin's eyes pierce straight through to my soul as he stares at me. "I don't think you could ever be rude."

"You're such a nice guy," I say as he shuts the door. I follow him into the kitchen as he picks up a knife.

"I'm not that nice." He lays his knife over a clove of garlic and pounds his fist down on it. "I can be mean."

I laugh lightly as I watch him mince the garlic. "You could never be mean."

He stops what he's doing and studies me. "Not to you."

I blush, and then scan the items on the counter. "What are you making?"

His smile is so wide it splits his face into two. "That's a surprise."

I take a seat on a barstool. "I love surprises."

"Hope you love gefilte fish."

I raise a brow. "Um, I hope you're kidding."

He laughs hard, setting his knife down. "You should have seen your face."

I crack a smile. "I thought you were serious. So, what are you making?" Now I need to know.

He steps closer to me, brushing some flyaway hairs away from my face. "I promise you'll love it."

I spread my legs so he can fit his lean frame in between them. "Promise?"

He kisses the tip of my nose. "Promise." He kisses me lightly on the lips, but I don't want him to stop.

I wrap my legs tighter around him, letting the kiss deepen naturally.

He finally breaks free, and opens his eyes, trained right on me. "You're so pretty. Do you even get how pretty you are?"

I smile, my cheeks flaming hot. "Thank you."

"You didn't answer my question."

My cheeks grow even hotter and I dip my head to stare at the floor. "No, I guess."

He sets two fingers under my chin, raising my head up so he can look into my eyes. "You're really fucking pretty."

I gaze into the depths of his eyes, wanting to memorize the color. "Thank you."

"I've always thought so," he whispers, and my mind wants to analyze that statement over and over again. "I got a great deal on a ribeye," he says, changing the subject so quickly I can't ask him to elaborate. He steps away from me to continue working.

"Oh yum," I say.

"I'm making it with a sweet potato puree, balsamic roasted mushrooms and sautéed sprouts. Do you like brussel sprouts?"

I nod. "I love them." I glance around his kitchen, looking at all the prep work he's doing. "You really didn't have to go through all of this trouble. I would have been okay with a pizza."

He stops straining the sweet potatoes, and stares at me. "First, no, you wouldn't have because once you taste this you'll love it so much more than pizza. Second, it's really not any trouble. I enjoy doing this."

"Can I help?"

He resumes straining the potatoes. "You can get us both a glass of wine?"

I smile. "Now that I can do. I'm really kind of hopeless in the kitchen."

"I bet that's not true."

I head to his cupboard, opening a few before he points to one which holds the wine glasses. I pull two down. "I don't have a skill for cooking, but I definitely am skilled at carrying on a conversation with the person doing the cooking."

Griffin's eyes light up like the Fourth of July. "I love that. And you can sit here and keep me company every time I cook."

His words almost speak of a future of us ending up together, and I let my mind wander there. I'm actually not mad at it. I can picture coming home from work, watching Griffin prepare a meal just for the two of us.

I kind of dig this future unfolding before my very eyes.

Griffin steps closer and takes the glass of wine I've poured for him. "You okay?" he asks me as he raises the glass to his lips and takes a sip. "You sort of went quiet on me."

I raise my own wine glass to my lips, smelling the nice aroma of the Pinot Noir. "I'm just thinking about sitting here and keeping you company every time you cook."

He sets his wine glass down. "I might need to kick you out of this kitchen." He takes my wine glass from my hand and sets it along the counter. He invades my space. "Because I'm not going to get much cooking done with you sitting here looking like a meal I'd like to devour instead."

My chest grows warm. "Griffin," I whisper right before he kisses me.

He wraps his arms around me, pulling me closer to him. "You have no idea," he whispers as he breaks the kiss. "No fucking clue."

"No clue about what?" I blink up at him.

He cups my cheek. "No clue about what I'd like to do to you."

I smile wide. "Will you feed me first?"

"Depends on what you'd like to eat." He's got this playful look in his eyes.

"How about dinner, and then I'll have you for dessert," I say, feeling brave.

He smoothes my hair back with his hand, bringing his lips mere inches from mine. "Only if I get to return the favor."

"Absolutely," I say before he kisses me once more.

Chapter 14

Griffin

Dinner took way too long to cook, and I'm sure it's because I'm already looking forward to dessert. When I opened the door tonight, and Anya stood on my front porch looking like any man's wet dream, I felt like the luckiest bastard on the planet.

Seriously.

She just doesn't get how pretty she is. How funny she is. How things just feel fucking right between us.

After dinner, Anya helped me clean the kitchen, despite my attempts to take on the task myself. She insisted, her determination shining through as she grabbed a dishcloth and started scrubbing. I love how nice she is. Most women might sit back and enjoy watching a man slave away for them, but not Anya. She wants to work as a team with me, just as she does at the brewery. Her collaborative spirit turns me on and makes me feel like we've got something real brewing between us.

As we work side by side, rinsing dishes and wiping down counters, I can't help but admire her. She moves with a graceful efficiency, her sleeves rolled up, revealing her slender arms. The way she glances over at me, with a playful smile dancing on her lips, makes my heart race. The kitchen's filled with the comforting sounds of running water and clinking dishes, and the scent of the delicious meal we just shared still lingers in the air.

Once the kitchen is spotless, Anya steps up to me, her eyes sparkling with mischief. She places her hand gently on my chest, sending a shiver down my spine. "I'm ready for dessert," she whispers, her voice a sultry promise. Her eyes lock onto mine for a fraction of a second, a silent conversation passing between us, before she crashes her lips to mine.

The kiss is electric. Her heart pounds against my chest as I wrap my arms around her, pulling her closer. The world outside fades away, leaving just the two of us in our little bubble of intimacy. Her fingers tangle in my hair, and I respond by deepening the kiss.

Our bodies press closer and I have no shame in pushing my hard cock against her. She responds by rubbing herself against it, causing me to groan into her mouth. Unable to stop myself, my hands glide down her body and sink into her round ass. I pull her against me, pushing my solid dick against her once more.

She breaks the kiss as her head falls back. "Griffin," she moans.

I take advantage of her exposed neck and move my lips down to it. Soft kisses soon become gentle nibbles and she moans against the tender bites. My fingers dig into her ass, wanting—no needing—more.

"Anya, I need to hear you say you want this. I need to know before I strip you naked and worship your sweet body that you want this as much as I do."

Her chest rises and falls rapidly, pushing her tits closer to my face as I wait for her to say what I desperately need to hear. She lifts her head, crashing her heated eyes with mine as her fingernails dig into my shoulders. "I want this, Griffin," she whispers, but damn I feel like she shouted it.

I'm breaking a promise I swore I wouldn't, but it no longer matters. I can't keep denying what I'm feeling.

What I want—Anya.

I easily lift her and she wraps her legs around me as I carry her to my bedroom. When we get inside, I kick the door closed behind us and allow her to slide down my body. I take a small step back and stare at her.

Her dark hair, wild from my fingers, falls in waves around her shoulders. Her lips are swollen from my kiss. Her skin's flushed from my touch.

"Fuck, you're gorgeous." I pull my shirt off, keeping my eyes pinned on her. "Strip."

She searches my face, processing what I've just told her. The sweet guy, the fix it guy, demanding her to strip. It's out of character for the person she knows, but the guy I am out of the bedroom and the guy I am *in* the bedroom are two different people.

I'm not full of sweet supportive words and encouragement. I'm desperate—*frantic*—feral in the bedroom.

"Don't make me tell you again," I say, folding my arms over my chest.

She snaps out of her thoughts and reaches behind her to unzip the dress she has on. It falls off her, pooling at her feet. My eyes travel down her body. Her hard nipples are visible through her white silk bra and I feel my cock press against the zipper of my jeans. I rub my hand against it as my eyes continue down her incredible body. Her white lace and silk panties are where my eyes stop as I let out a rugged breath.

"Fucking stunning. Take your bra off and slowly slide your panties down your long legs."

She grins as her eyes travel down my chest to my jeans. "Take your pants off."

I step up to her and sink my fingers roughly into her hair, pulling her head back so she's looking up at me. "I'm in charge here. You don't tell me what to do. Got it?" She visibly swallows and tries to nod her head, but my hold on her hair doesn't allow it. "Tell me you understand," I demand.

"I understand," she whispers as her eyes darken with lust.

I step back and nod for her to continue. This time she doesn't say anything. Like a good girl, she reaches back and unclasps her bra, allowing it to slide down her arms. She drops it on the floor and I nearly go down with it when I see her perfect fucking tits for the first time.

"Fuck, I'm going to come all over those," I say, poking my tongue out to wet my dry lips.

Her eyes glaze over as she bites gently on her lower lip. She likes this side of me and that turns me on even more.

She hooks her fingers into her panties and slowly pushes them down her legs, bending at the waist. Her tits bounce from the movement and I can no longer wait. As she reaches her ankles, I unbutton my jeans and push them down my legs, kicking off my shoes. She steps back, leaving her panties in front of her and I step forward, leaving my jeans behind me.

"I've fantasized about this moment more times than I'd care to admit, but it was nothing compared to this. You standing naked in front of me. Your face flushed with want. Your nipples hard and begging for attention. And if I had to guess, I'd bet your pussy is dripping wet with need." I rub my hard dick through my boxer-briefs and take a step closer to her. "Look what you do to me." Her eyes glance down at my hand and slide back up to mine. "I've been walking around with a hard dick just thinking about you."

"Touch me, Griffin, please."

I grin as I push my briefs off, freeing my cock. "Oh Anya, hearing you beg is fucking hot. We're going to have so much fun." I wrap my hand around my dick and slowly pump as I stare at her. "I think you need to take care of what you've created. Get on your knees, Anya."

She doesn't argue, she drops to her knees and it's fucking hot looking down at her. I continue to pump my dick with one hand and with the other I sink my fingers into her silky hair.

"Wrap those sexy lips around my dick and suck me off. Finish what you've started," I groan.

Her eyes lift to mine as she places her hands on my thighs. I hiss at the touch but she keeps her eyes on mine as her tongue pokes out and she licks the head of my cock.

"Fuck, take me into your mouth," I hiss.

Her eyes drift closed as her lips wrap around me and she takes me into her mouth. I remove my hand when it hits her lips and add it with the other in her hair. She slowly moves against me, but I give her a bit of time to get used to my size.

I tighten my hold on her hair, unable to take it anymore. "Faster, Anya. Don't fucking tease me."

My words have her moving faster, but I help her find the speed I need by pumping my hips and moving her head with my hold on her hair.

"Yes, fuck, just like that. Use your hand for what you can't fit in that hot little mouth of yours." She immediately wraps her hand around my shaft and finds the perfect fast rhythm. "Oh fuck yes. Swallow me whole," I groan.

I look down at the sight before me and I nearly come down her throat. My cock's sliding in and out of her mouth. Her body moves along with her bobbing head. Her hair falls around her. It's a sight I will fantasize about long after tonight.

She's sucking me off like she's a starving woman and I'm her last meal and it's fucking incredible.

"I'm not going to last much longer and that's your fault. You've had me on the verge of coming for weeks now and I can't fight it anymore," I moan out.

She uses her free hand and cups my balls, causing me to pull her hair harder as I jerk my hips forward. She doesn't gag or react, she takes it and I drop my head back allowing her to finish me off. My body tightens and my legs shake as my release fights its way out.

"Yes, fuck Anya, I'm going to come. Take it all, drink me down," I hiss.

She scrapes her teeth against me and I lose it. I come hard and fast and she does in fact take every single drop I have to give.

When I finish I pull her off me and she looks up and licks her lips. "Fuck," I say, pulling her up and lifting her naked body into my arms. I crash my lips to hers and we both moan at the contact. I can feel her wet pussy against me and now that she's taken care of me, I need to show her just how good I'm gonna take care of her. How badly I want to take care of her.

I break the kiss and rest my forehead against her. "Fucking amazing." I kiss her nose and grin. "Your turn." I lay her on the bed and look down at her. She looks angelic laying there and I'm about to show her the devil.

I reach down and pull my shirt off the floor and twist it while holding both ends, so it's a long thinner version of itself. Her eyes are searching mine as I grin down at her.

"The five main human senses are sight, touch, smell, hearing, and taste. Take one away and the others become more enhanced. I'm going to take away your sight and you'll experience touch like never before. You'll hear more intently, wondering where I am and what I'm doing. You'll smell our arousal and when I'm finished you'll taste yours better than you ever have. Just by simply taking your sight, I'm going to make you experience ecstasy like never before."

"Damn, Griffin, I had no idea you were so dominant," she says.

"I'm sexual, Anya and if getting both of us intense orgasms makes me dominant, I'll fucking wear the title proudly." I kiss her soft lips and look down at her. I've yet to touch her and it's driving me wild. "I'm gonna blindfold you now because I need to learn your every curve."

She doesn't argue and allows me to tie my shirt over her eyes. I stand back and look at her and a ragged breath escapes me. She looks fucking sexy as hell.

I climb onto the bed and it dips with my weight which causes her to grab onto the comforter. I smile, loving that already she's experiencing what it's like to have her sight taken. I run my hands down from her slender neck, over her arms, and back to her chest. Her chest is rising and falling rapidly, partly out of excitement and partly out of fear of not knowing what's coming next. It's a huge turn-on.

I use my thumbs to trace her hard nipples and her back arches off the bed at the simple touch. "It's more intense when you don't expect it," I whisper, pinching both nipples. She cries out and I grin as I lean down and finally suck on the soft skin of her tits.

"Oh God," she moans, moving beneath me.

I lick, suck, and bite on her soft flushed skin as my fingers continue to play with her nipples. She reaches out, feeling for me and grabs onto my forearms. I move my hands and grab hers, pinning them to her side while I suck on her nipples.

"Yes," she cries out, moving her hips, rubbing herself against me.

I smile, and bite both her nipples before moving down her body. I kiss my way down to her pussy and when I reach it, I settle between her legs, making sure they are wide open. I drag my fingers through her wet folds and groan.

"Fuck, you're dripping wet." I press a kiss to her pussy and even though she can't see me, I look up at her. "This is what I do to you. The confusion you felt was because you didn't want to listen to what your body was telling you." I drag my tongue from her entrance to her clit and flick it with my tongue. "Your body is telling you that you want me, that you need me to steal your orgasm. That you need me." I lick at her again and say, "Tell me you're no longer fucking confused."

"I'm not confused, Griffin. Please," she begs.

I hum against her pussy. "That's right, beg for what you want." She doesn't say anything and I move away. "Wait, no, please Griffin. Please make me come."

"Fuck yes," I hiss.

I attack her pussy like a parched traveler finding an oasis in the desert. Her taste coats my tongue and I ravish on the sweetest thing I've ever tasted. Licking, sucking, biting, while her moans and cries echo around us. I wrap my lips around her and bite down on her sensitive clit and she screams out of pain and pleasure. I frantically lick at her clit and then plunge two fingers inside her.

"Fuck, oh my God," she shouts.

I hum against her as my fingers fuck her tight pussy. She cries out again and it vibrates through me. She's close, I can feel her tightening on my fingers and I'm ready. I curl my fingers and suck on her clit as she screams above me. I use my free hand and reach up, pinching her nipples and she jumps with surprise.

"Griffin, oh yes, I'm going to come," she shouts.

I didn't need the warning, but it's fucking hot listening to her voice so thick with arousal.

I fuck her with my fingers and nibble down on her clit and that's it. That's all it takes for her to explode around me.

"Griffin, fuck," she screams.

I lap at her wetness as she rides out her release and when she calms, I climb up her body. I slam my mouth to hers. She moans as she tastes herself and I moan along with her.

After several minutes I break the kiss and run my thumb along her bottom lip. "That was fucking hot." I press my thumb against her lips and smile. "Wait until you find out what it feels like for me to fuck you with that blindfold." I remove my thumb and reach for a condom. "Beg me for it."

Fuck, I didn't know if I'd be able to be myself with Anya like this, but it's the most erotic experience of my life and my dick hasn't even been inside her yet.

Chapter 15

Anya

I need a moment to breathe. To react to what just went down between Griffin and I, pun intended.

That was quite possibly the greatest thing that has ever happened to me in my life. I've never felt like that before. I've never experienced anything that intense in my life.

Who knew it could be like that?

I sure as heck didn't. And we haven't even had sex yet, but there's something about Griffin's dirty mouth that keeps my body pulsing with need.

When he demanded I strip for him, I'd never been more turned on. Seeing his dick, and the many, *many* inches of him, had me wet before I even sank to my knees. Feeling him in my mouth, the way his eyes bore into mine was too much. I would have given my life to please him.

But nothing could have prepared me for how it felt when he went down on me. How good it felt.

I just had an orgasm like two seconds ago, and yet, my body is still just as needy. "Griffin," I groan out.

He gently runs his fingers down the side of my body. "Anya, I've thought about you beneath me like this for a long fucking time."

Is that true?

I want to ask him for how long, but before I can he kisses me. And it isn't like any kiss we've shared before. This one is more passionate. More fervent. More everything.

I don't want it to end.

When the kiss breaks, I beg, "Please let me see you."

I can feel his dick hardening against me, and he removes his shirt from my eyes, using it to tie my wrists together above my head. "Keep your hands above your head."

"So bossy," I tease, and his eyes darken.

"You have no idea."

Who knew Griffin was like this in the bedroom? It's a complete turn on, and makes me want to see how bossy he can get. It also makes me wonder what he'd do if I don't adhere to his commands.

Would he spank me?

Would I like it?

He leans back, studying my body. "You've got a perfect fucking body." He trails kisses across my heated skin.

My back arches off the bed, needing to be closer to him. "It's yours, take it," I tell him before he kisses me once more.

He growls as he finishes the kiss, getting up to his knees so he can study my body better. "It's like my own personal wonderland, and I don't know where to start."

I blush.

He fists his dick as he kneels between my legs. "I think I might fuck those perfect tits first."

I groan, twisting slightly on the bed. "No, please," I beg, needing to feel him inside me.

He tsks me. "What did I say about who's in charge?"

"You're in charge," I moan out, my body growing with desire.

"That's right. Don't you forget it." He pumps his dick with his fist and bites his lower lip as his gaze travels down my body. "I can fuck your tits later, I've waited almost a damn lifetime to get inside your pussy." He runs the engorged head of his dick through my wetness, pressing it firmly against my clit before running it back down, stopping at my entrance. "Are you on the pill?"

I shake my head. "No."

"Tomorrow, you'll call the doctor, get on the pill." He rips open the condom packet with his teeth, and I watch as he rolls it over his thick length. "Now spread these long legs."

I do as he says as he presses his dick against my opening. He pushes in, slowly, letting my body acclimate to his enormous size.

And then he starts pumping, in and out, turning my body on with each thrust of his hips.

"Griffin," I moan out, unable to believe this is really happening between us. And that it's so *so* good.

He knows just where to touch me to make me cry out in pleasure. Knows just how to pound deep inside me to make me scream out in ecstasy. I'm so close to unraveling I can barely breathe.

"Don't stop," I whine, and Griffin just keeps going, hammering away inside me.

"You like my fucking hard cock, huh? You like teasing me with your little outfits. Making me hard every fucking day I see you."

I gaze into his eyes. "I...I..." I stutter. I had no clue I was doing this to him. "I didn't mean to," I whisper.

"Anya, you have no idea what you do to me."

"What do I do to you?"

He lowers his body to where the majority of his weight presses down on me. I love it. "You turn me on every time I fucking see you. Do you know how difficult it is to work with a hard on?"

I giggle lightly. "I didn't know."

"Now you do," he says before crushing his lips to mine and picking up speed.

Our bodies move together, creating enough friction along my clit to have my body racing toward another orgasm. I've never had more than one orgasm in the span of one evening before.

When I knocked on Griffin's door this evening, I never expected for this to happen. But I'm glad it is.

I want him.

And that thought terrifies me and excites me.

I wrap my legs around him, keeping him close as our tongues tangle together. "I'm coming," I shout out into the darkness of Griffin's bedroom.

"That's it. Come all over me, Anya."

Hearing his dirty words sends me spiraling over the edge. My breaths come out in pants as my body tightens around him, my orgasm crashing over me in waves.

"Fuck, I feel you coming on my cock. Can't hold on," he groans out, and his body shakes above me as his orgasm slams into him.

It's completely gorgeous the way he looks when he's getting off. Makes me want to memorize the moment.

As soon as our bodies have calmed, and he's already cleaning up, tossing the condom into the garbage can, he smiles. "We'll definitely need to do that a few more times."

"A few more hundred times," I say with a laugh.

After he's cleaned up he lays next to me, propped up on his elbow and looking down on me. "We should keep this a secret until we figure out how to tell people."

I nod. "I couldn't agree more," I say, wondering what my brothers will think about me dating Griffin.

Are we dating?

Chapter 16

Griffin

Anya spent the night, last night, and waking up with her in my arms was something I didn't even know I needed until I opened my eyes. My arms wrapped around her delicate body. Her face inches from mine. The way her hair splayed across the pillow. Damn, I didn't want to move and disturb such a peaceful moment.

That may be what it is I'm needing or craving—peace.

I never experienced a sense of peace growing up. I was constantly walking on eggshells, always in a persistent state of nervousness. The only time I felt my body relax was when I was at the Atwood's and even that was just temporary because I knew I'd eventually have to leave.

But this morning, waking up with Anya, I felt a peace I've never experienced before and it was amazing.

She left this morning, after I made her come twice, and it was not easy to let her go. I wanted us both to call out of work and spend the day in bed, but she reminded me we have a party tonight. After a long goodbye kiss, I watched her pull out of my driveway and my heart sank. One night together and I feel like I can't breathe without her.

That's why I'm equal parts excited and nervous to be at Atta Boy today. I can't wait to see her, to have her near me, but that also means I'll be seeing Callum. I'll be seeing all the Atwood's for Christ's sake and I honestly don't know how I'm going to react.

I broke my promise to Callum, and while there was no possible way around it, the weight of my actions sits heavily on my shoulders. The connection I feel to Anya is unavoidable, an intense need stronger than anything I've ever experienced before. It's not just attraction; it's something deeper, something that pulls me toward her with an irresistible force.

Yet, I know Callum won't understand. He'll see me as the guy who betrayed his trust and took advantage of his little sister. He'll look at me with disappointment and anger, unable to see the depth of my feelings for Anya. In his eyes, I'll be nothing more than a promise-breaker.

The thought of losing my friendship with Callum gnaws at me. We've been through so much together, shared countless memories and built a bond that felt unbreakable. But now, that bond is at risk. I've worked hard to get where I am, and Callum's influence is significant. If he turns against me, I'll be left scrambling to pick up the pieces of my shattered career.

I won't be the same person if that happens and I won't be the same person if I lose Anya.

I'm cornered and I don't know how to get out.

But, I told Anya we should keep this a secret and thankfully she agreed. So, until I figure out how things will play out, my relationship with her will be kept in the shadows.

"Hey, Griffin," Tripp says, slinking into the kitchen.

"You're late," I say, keeping my back to him as I chop potatoes.

"I overslept and Anya took too long in the bathroom."

I spin around and stare at him with narrowed eyes. "So you're blaming being irresponsible on your sister?"

I'll be damned if I'm going to allow him to put the blame on anyone, especially Anya.

"I'm not blaming her. I'm just saying it's part of the reason I'm late." He moves to stand next to me and smiles up at me. "What's going on with you two?"

I turn back to chopping potatoes and shake my head. "We're friends and we work together. Nothing more to it, Tripp. Don't try to avoid what's going on with you by focusing on nonsense that doesn't exist."

"Hey."

I spin around and see Anya standing there and my heart sinks. I know from the look of hurt in her eyes she heard what I said to Tripp.

"Why aren't you telling her she's late?" Tripp says, shaking his head.

"Tripp, if you don't get out of my sight I'm going to end up hurting you. Go set up the tables for lunch," I say, keeping my eyes locked with Anya's. He slowly starts to walk toward the door and the anger I feel with myself continues to get misplaced. "Now, God damn it."

Once he leaves, I move slowly toward Anya and rest my hand on her cheek. She forces a smile and nods. "I know."

"You weren't meant to hear that. I was trying to get him to focus on himself. I'm sorry. This is brand new with us and honestly, I just want to keep you all to myself right now."

She searches my eyes and a genuine smile graces her face. "We both decided to keep this between us for now. You didn't do anything wrong."

I push her against the wall behind the door. I crash my lips to hers and we both let out a soft moan at the reconnection. It's hard and fast, but full of promise for what lies ahead.

When I pull back, I grin down at her, running my thumb over her bottom lip. "That's something I've wanted to do in this kitchen for a long time."

"Just kiss me?" she questions with mischief in her eyes.

I push my knee between her legs and grab her wrists, pinning them above her head. "There's a lot I want to do to you in this kitchen and I promise you I will."

The door opens, hitting me in the back and I quickly let go of her. "Damn, sorry," Callum says, walking into the kitchen. "Wait, what the hell are you guys doing behind the door?"

"I dropped my earring and Griffin was helping me look, but I found it. I'll be back later to check in on the menu," she says, walking out of the kitchen.

It takes a lot of self-control to hide my smile as I watch her round ass as she walks away. She protected this secret thing between us the same way I did and it makes me relax a little bit.

"Tripp is out there working already. He said you told him to come in," Callum says, leaning against the counter.

"Yeah, he wanted to pick up some extra cash and I told him he could help me today. That's cool, right?"

"It's great. Maybe he's finally starting to take an interest in the brewery." I've gone back to prepping and Callum moves to stand by me. "Listen, I know we haven't had time to talk lately, but I want you to know I see you going out of your way to help Anya and Tripp. You're a good friend, Griff. Sometimes there's just not enough time in the day to do it all and it's nice to know that you're there to help when I can't."

If he only knew how I was helping his sister.

Yep, I'm an asshole.

"Helping Tripp is easy. I get to be the big brother I never was," I say, forcing a laugh.

He chuckles, crossing his muscular arms. "I know, helping him is easier than helping Anya. She's a lot to handle."

Anger and guilt wrap around me and I slide my eyes to his. "I'm not helping her, I believe in her dream and I'm part of what is making it a reality. That's not a burden, Cal, it's an honor."

He nods, taken back a little by my comment. It's not something I'd usually say to him, but I'm beginning to see that Anya isn't the only one that sees me as the 'fix it' guy.

"I appreciate that, Griff. You're not just my best friend, but you're a fucking stand-up guy. I wouldn't trust my sister with anyone else."

With that he leaves the kitchen and I'm left feeling like I'm being torn in two.

Chapter 17

Anya

I head into the back office to work a bit before the party tonight. There's a lot to be done, and I pride myself as I get busy.

"Hey, there's a call for you on line one," Tripp says, sticking his head in my office.

I nod at him with a smile and answer the call. "Hello," I say into the phone.

"Hi, this is Xander Reeves, mayor of Magnolia Ridge."

I giggle lightly into the phone. "Yes, Mayor Reeves, I know who you are."

"I'm having a few county officials coming into town to have an important meeting, and I'd like for Atta Boy to host it."

I quickly grab my pen and calendar, my mind already racing with ideas. "Absolutely, we'd love to do that for you," I respond enthusiastically, trying to keep my excitement in check.

As I take down the details for the event, I realize this will be one of the biggest parties we'll have this year. This event could catapult Atta Boy into the national spotlight. If everything goes right, our brewery could be featured in a national tourism magazine, showcasing us as a must-visit destination. I imagine the influx of tourists, the bustling crowds eager to taste our craft beers, and the neighboring cities adding us to their 'Things to Do in Magnolia Ridge' lists. The potential for press coverage is enormous, with journalists and bloggers sharing their experiences and spreading the word.

We can't screw this up.

As soon as I hang up, I rush down to Callum's office to tell him the good news. He's out of his office chair the minute he sees what a big deal this is as well.

"We'll have to really impress them," he says, pacing his office floor. His eyes meet mine. "Seriously Anya, good work."

This is the first time Callum has ever acknowledged the good work I'm doing around here. I definitely can't screw this up.

"Hey, what's got you so excited?" Paxton asks as he steps into the office.

I relay the info to my brother, and his eyes fill with excitement as well. He leans his head out the door, shouting, "Hey Shep, come hear this," he says, and Shepherd walks into the office.

After relaying the information to yet another brother of mine, the office becomes a hodgepodge of bustling activity.

My brothers can't contain their excitement as news of the upcoming party spreads to Brock and Tripp. Soon, the whole staff is buzzing with enthusiasm. As I head up to the kitchen to tell Griffin personally, my nerves get the best of me. Everything with him is so new and thrilling, I'm not sure how to act around him at work. It's crazy, but I can't stop thinking about him, and I definitely want him to keep kissing me.

I never in a million years saw myself falling for a guy like Griffin, but now that I am, I can't stop the speed at which I'm falling. He's electric, and our chemistry is off the charts. Just thinking about the things he can do with his tongue excites me.

I step into the back prep area, trying to steady my racing heart. "Did you hear?" I ask him, my voice barely steady.

Griffin's smile is wide and infectious. "This is going to be amazing."

"We have to come up with the perfect menu. We really need to impress these people," I say, trying to focus on the task at hand. I notice Griffin's hands inching closer to me, and I can tell he wants to touch me. He stops himself, though, realizing we aren't alone.

"Crazy news, right?" Shep says, slapping a hand on Griffin's shoulder. "Anya, let me know how many servers I should schedule for the event."

I nod, my mind already planning. "I will. I'm about to go to my office and start planning before the party tonight." I turn my attention back to Griffin, feeling a rush of warmth. "We're all ready to go for tonight, right?"

He nods, his eyes twinkling. "Yep."

As I turn to leave, I feel Griffin's gaze follow me. I can't help but glance back, catching his smile. I hurry back to the confines of my office to prepare for tonight. My mind races with possibilities about the upcoming party, but I keep getting interrupted with the way Griffin made me feel last night.

And how I want him to make me feel that way again —tonight.

<hr>

I'm currently on my knees, gazing up at Griffin as he slips his jeans down his body. The party ended just a mere forty-five minutes ago, and after everyone went home, Griffin stopped by my office to walk me to my car.

We didn't make it very far.

Instead he kissed me, and one thing led to another that ended with me on my knees.

He pulls his dick out of his briefs, and I lick my lips. "You're so hungry for it, aren't you?"

I nod like a good girl, and give him my best pouty face when he doesn't bring his dick any closer. "Please," I beg of him, wanting to suck him off more than anything.

I'm turned on, and there's a throbbing between my thighs that no amount of clenching satisfies.

"Open wide," he says as he feeds me his dick.

I close my mouth around his engorged head, and suck on him, hollowing out my cheeks. His eyes roll into the back of his head as his mouth falls open.

"Fuck," he groans as I keep sucking on him.

I wouldn't call myself a pro dick sucker, but what I am doing to Griffin he apparently loves. He fists his hands in my long hair, and guides my mouth up and down his thick shaft.

The fact we're still here at work makes my body tingle with excitement. We could get into so much trouble if we're caught, and that makes me pause briefly.

"You okay?" Griffin asks me, and I gaze into his soft brown eyes.

I nod, continuing my assault on his dick. I keep sucking, wanting more than anything to please him. To make him come undone like he makes me.

It's insane that I've already got such strong feelings for him. Right? I keep sucking as his hand fists tightly in my hair.

"That's right," he breathes out. "Make me come."

I keep going, fueled by the desire swimming in his eyes.

"You suck me off so good, Anya," he whispers out into the darkness surrounding my office. "I'm so close," he shouts, and I grip him tighter, wanting him to come. Wanting to taste everything he's got to give.

The way he looks at me turns me on as he holds on to me tighter. His face morphs into one of pure pleasure as he comes deep down my throat.

I keep sucking, milking his release as his eyes stay connected with mine, bringing us that much closer.

"Come to my place," he whispers as soon as his body starts to calm.

I rise from where I was kneeling on the floor, and wipe my bottom lip. "I should really get home and get some sleep. I've got a ton to do tomorrow."

Griffin steps closer, after cleaning himself up, and zipping up his jeans. "You can sleep at my place."

I park a hand on my hip. "You know we won't get any sleeping done."

He wraps his arms around my waist, bringing me closer. "We'll get a little bit of sleeping done."

I smile against his lips. "Okay," I say before he kisses me.

I'm beginning to realize there's nothing I won't do for Griffin.

Chapter 18

Griffin

Anya follows behind me as we drive to my house. It was harder than I imagined it would be working so closely today and having to hide my feelings. My body was burning with need and each time our paths crossed, it just intensified.

Breaking my promise to Callum is meaningless when it's just Anya and me. The connection, the attraction, the want, overpowers everything else.

After another fucking amazing blow job, there was no way I was letting her walk away. I want her waking up next to me again as much as I want to hear her screaming my name.

I pull into my driveway, hop out of my truck, and walk to the tailgate as she pulls in behind me. As she closes her car door, my eyes lock with hers just before the headlights of her car turn off and the moonlight is the only thing shining. I meet her as she steps in front of her car and slam my mouth to hers. A moan escapes her and the slight breeze carries it away.

Her fingers dig into my shoulders and her legs squeeze together to try to relieve some of the tension she must be feeling.

I break the kiss and my eyes bounce between hers. "You need relief?"

"Yes," she breathes out, nodding her head.

I push my knee between her legs, grateful she's wearing a dress. My greedy girl rubs her aching pussy against my leg and I growl, pulling her head back by her hair. "I love the idea of making you beg me for what you want. The idea of watching you squirm trying to relieve some of the pressure that's building between your legs. Especially because I'm the one causing it. I fucking love that idea, but I think we've both suffered long enough today. I'm going to give you what you need but I'm going to do it right here."

Her eyes snap to mine, widening. "Outside?" She looks around. "But what if someone sees us?"

I push my knee against her center and she moans. "The idea of being caught adds to the excitement, Anya. The thought that someone could look out their window or walk by and see me buried deep inside your wet pussy, makes it even more thrilling." I move my hands down her sexy body and push up her dress, keeping my eyes locked with hers. My fingers hook around her panties and I push them down. As they fall to her ankles, I lift her, placing her on the hood of her car, which is no longer hot from the drive. I grab her panties and shove them into my pocket.

She holds tightly onto my upper arms for support and possibly because she's a little nervous about being caught. It turns me on even more and I didn't think that was possible.

I lean forward and kiss her neck, sucking lightly on her soft skin. Her soft sounds mix in with the sound of crickets chirping and the breeze rustling the leaves. My lips trail down her neck and when I reach the top of her dress, I use my teeth to pull it down over her perfect tits.

"Are you trying to tease me by not wearing a bra?"

I bite down on her hard nipples and she arches her back, pushing them further into my face.

"Yes," she whispers.

My fingers dig into her thighs as I search her face. "Be careful, Anya. We've agreed to keep this a secret and if you go around teasing me, I won't be held responsible for what I do or who's around when I do it."

"Fuck," she breathes out.

I push her legs further apart and make quick work of getting my jeans and boxers down just past my ass. My dick presses against her center and she tries pushing herself closer.

"Reach into my pocket and pull out the condom I have and roll it on me," I demand.

She doesn't hesitate and does what I say. When her small hands lightly touch my cock, it jerks and I grab it to help her. She slowly pushes the condom on and I could come just from this alone.

I take a deep breath to get control of myself and yank her ass closer to the edge of the hood. I rub my dick through her wet folds and she braces herself with her hands behind her.

"Griffin," she moans.

"That's it, say my name loudly so everyone knows who you belong to," I say, slamming my thick cock into her pussy.

I keep my focus on her pussy gripping my dick as I drive into her. The cool air blows past us and the moonlight shines down, giving me just enough light to see how fucking beautiful she looks. I slam into her and she lets out a loud cry of pleasure.

It spurs me on and I fuck her hard and fast. Both of us making sounds that could attract wild animals at this point. Not to mention catch my neighbors attention.

Part of me wants that to happen, but another part of me would kill someone who laid their eyes on my half-naked girl, while my dick is buried deep inside her.

I reach between us and rub her clit with my thumb. She shouts as her body arches off the car.

It's fucking stunning.

"Griffin, I'm so close," she moans.

"I feel you tightening around me. Don't fight it, Anya. Let everyone know how I make you feel."

I rub her clit faster as I continue to slam into her. Her exposed tits bounce in the moonlight, her sounds echoing around us, and her pussy gripping me hard. It won't be long after I take her release that she takes mine.

I pinch her sensitive bundle and slam into her. She shouts my name as her orgasm rips through her. As I watch her, she steals another piece of me.

"Fuck, Griffin," she shouts.

"That's it, Anya, come on me and take my orgasm."

I dive into her a few more times and I can't fight it anymore. My balls tighten and my body stills as I come hard, digging my fingers into her soft flesh.

"Fuck," I groan.

I pull her against me and we hold onto each other as we catch our breath. I can feel her heart racing and I'm sure she can feel mine.

"That was hot," she whispers, kissing my neck.

"You're hot," I say, kissing her soft lips.

She smiles against them and I slightly pull back, raising an eyebrow. "We didn't even make it into the house," she says with a laugh.

I grin and pull the top of her dress back up to cover her perfect tits. "That's because the connection between us is so intense we can't control ourselves." I pull myself out of her causing us both to flinch. "Plus, my neighbors got a free show."

We both laugh, but she quickly stops. "Wait, do you think they really saw us?" she asks, looking around.

I dispose of the condom quickly, and button my jeans as I help her off the hood of her car. "I doubt it, but it would've been a hell of a show."

She smiles at me, wrapping her arms around my neck. "This side of you is sexy as hell."

I lift her and she wraps her legs around me. "Such a dirty girl. I think it's time to clean you up in the shower." I kiss her quickly as I walk to the front door. "After I get you good and dirty."

Anya and I did in fact only get a little sleep last night. Neither of us regretted that this morning. The only thing I regret was letting her leave. I know she had a lot to do today, but I wanted her to stay, because waking up with her is euphoria.

Unfortunately, she left and I've been lying in bed reliving the last few days, with a smile on my face.

My phone disrupts my thoughts and I sigh, grabbing it off the nightstand.

> Paxton: Sunday dinner at Mom and Dad's. Everyone must be there.

> Brock: Aren't we always there?

> Paxton: Check the text, dipshit. There are others included.

> I never turn down an invite to an Atwood Sunday dinner.

> Tripp: Who else is included? I don't have the numbers saved.

> Paxton: That means you don't need to have them saved.

> Anya: Why are my friends invited?

My heart races as she replies. Her friends? I know we're keeping this a secret but damn that word *friend* hurts.

> Paxton: Lake is my friend who happens to be dating your friend.

I shake my head, feeling like a fool. Of course she's not talking about me. I'm Callum's friend, not hers.

Shepherd: Obviously I'll be there.

Lake: Willow has told me about these dinners and I'm excited and nervous to be there. Thanks for the invite, I think.

Paxton: You haven't lived until you've experienced an Atwood Sunday dinner.

Brock: Millie, are you coming?

Hartford: Maybe you should've texted that to her in private, haha.

Tripp: Millie? From the bookstore? Why?

Paxton: Tripp, don't be an asshole. Millie and Hartford are friends and Brock is dating her. You'd know this stuff if you were around a little more.

Anya: He was just asking, no need to get upset. Seems like everyone will be there, sounds like a fun day.

Callum: Do Mom and Dad know you've invited a house full?

Paxton: No, I thought we'd surprise them and not have enough food for everyone.

Hartford: Paxton, stop. Yes, of course they know.

Shepherd: I'm bringing extra beer.

Do you want me to make anything?

Callum: Do you want to piss off my mom?

> Anya: Why are all my brothers such assholes all the time? A simple, no thanks, would've been great.

I chuckle, loving how Anya comes to my defense.

I leave that group message and pull up Anya's name.

> It's hot seeing you get defensive.

> Anya: LOL they just need to chill out.

> This is going to be the first time we're around everyone. You gonna be able to keep your hands off me?

> Anya: You might want to worry about that because I'm not going to be wearing panties.

> I will fuck you in the bathroom with no regrets. Don't tease me.

> Anya: I guess you won't know if I'm teasing or not. See you later ;)

This is going to be a long night.

Chapter 19

Anya

I wake up bright and early on Sunday morning to help my mother prepare all of the food for dinner. The sun is just starting to rise, casting a warm, golden glow through the kitchen windows. Last night, my mother and I stayed up super late making chocolates just for today. The kitchen still carries the sweet, lingering aroma of melted chocolate, and there are trays of beautifully crafted truffles and bonbons arranged on the counter.

As we chop vegetables and season the roast, the room fills with the comforting sounds of sizzling pans and the rhythmic chop of knives. I ask my mother why we are going all out, but she just smiles, her eyes twinkling with a hint of mischief, and says, "No reason." Her cryptic response only piques my curiosity further.

Tripp stumbles into the kitchen a while later, and gives our mother a peck on the cheek. "Smells good," he mumbles, and it's apparent he's had a rough night.

"Tripp, be a dear and help your father get the sleeve for the table. We've got a full house tonight," my mother says.

"I still don't know why we've invited so many people," Tripp says, heading out of the kitchen most likely in search of our father to help him set up the dining room.

"Our home is always open," she hollers after him.

I smile as I continue to chop the carrots. "Does he seem a lot more angry lately?"

My mother opens the oven to check on the roast. "He's dealing with something." She shuts the oven. "I just wish he'd tell somebody what that thing is."

I nod. "Griffin agreed to talk to him."

My mother beams. "Griffin is such a good man."

I try not to look too affected by her words. Like we haven't seen each other naked. "Sure," I say, absentmindedly. "He's nice."

My mother's obviously not buying it, but she doesn't press the matter for which I'm thankful for. "Hartford and Paxton should be here soon." My mother appears almost giddy at the idea of them showing up.

I park a hand on my hip. "What's really going on?"

My mother can't contain her excitement. "I'm not telling you much, all I know is Hartford and Paxton have an announcement."

My heart picks up in my chest. "You think Paxton proposed?"

My mother swats me with a towel. "I don't know. Hopefully it's that and not him telling us he knocked her up."

I laugh lightly. "It's not like Hartford is some one-night stand. He loves her. They obviously belong together." I'm so happy for my brother.

"I know." My mother almost looks like she could cry at any moment. "Honestly, I'd be over the moon if Hartford's got a bun in the oven."

We can't finish our conversation because my brothers, Callum and Shepherd, enter the kitchen. They both kiss our mother on the cheek, glance around the kitchen looking for scraps, and say their hellos.

"How's the party planning going for the mayor's thing?" Callum asks me, always all business.

"No, absolutely not," our mother scolds. "No business talk today."

Callum rolls his eyes, but continues looking at me, waiting for my response.

"I'm all over it. The party will be amazing. Mayor Reeves is going to get a small article in the local paper about the brewery this week, before the event. I already sent him all the promotional material."

Shepherd wraps an arm around my shoulder. "Have I ever told you that you're my favorite sister?"

"I'm your only sister."

He steps away from me, grabbing a slice of an apple Mom's cutting to prepare the apple pie and pops it into his mouth. "Still my favorite."

I laugh as Hartford and Paxton waltz into the kitchen. After everyone's said their hellos, Hartford steps up closer to me. "I heard a secret about you," she sing-songs, and my heart nearly plummets into my stomach.

"Secret?" I ask as Griffin decides at this very moment to walk into the kitchen. "What secret?"

Griffin's eyes meet mine, and my heart thumps wildly in my chest. "Hey," he whispers to me first before he gets torn away by Callum and Shep.

I can't even say hey back, because I return my attention back to Hartford. "What secret?"

"I heard somebody's making a name for herself as the head party planner at Atta Boy."

A sense of relief washes over me. Phew. I can breathe.

"Oh, right," I say, trying my best to smile. "Yes."

"Is the party in here?" Lake says, holding Willow's hand.

After everyone has said hello, and a few of the people, Griffin included, have left the kitchen, I'm left standing with my mother, Willow, and Hartford.

"Wonder when Millie's coming?" Hartford says, checking the time on her phone. "I can't believe her and Brock just started dating."

"I don't think they're technically dating. I think Brock is using the words, 'seeing each other'," I say, using air-quotes.

Tripp walks into the kitchen, and spots that it's just us girls in here and immediately walks right back out.

"What was all that about?" Hartford asks.

155

"Something's going on with him. He's been super grumpy lately. More than usual." I finish the carrots and hand them off to my mother.

"You know," Hartford starts. "Shep has been extra grumpy too. Ever since he's been home."

"Really?" my mother and I say in unison.

Willow chimes in with, "Maybe they've both got girl troubles."

Hartford leans her hip against the counter. "Paxton did say Shepherd hooked up with his neighbor over Christmas." Hartford glances at my mother whose face has fallen flat. "Sorry, Carol. You know what I mean."

We all laugh, minus my mother. My mother nearly swats her hand in the air. "I don't pretend to think my men aren't out being men."

Hartford's eyes go wide, and her cheeks blush. "Not Paxton," she says in a rush, and we all laugh harder, even my mother this time. "Seriously, we're abstaining from sexual..." her words fall away as she appears she's making the conversation worse.

"We all know you have sex," I say. "We read your article."

"Anya," Hartford nearly yells at the top of her lungs. "Oh god," she covers her face, "I can't believe you just said that around your mother." She faces my mother. "Carol, I'm sorry."

Mom only laughs harder. "Girls, as much as I've enjoyed this, get out of my kitchen."

Hartford spins on her heels quickly. "Gladly."

"I haven't talked to you in forever," Willow grabs my arm as we walk out of the kitchen and onto the back patio where everyone is sitting. "I'm sorry I've been so absent. Things with Lake are going really well."

I stop walking so I can hug my best friend. "I'm really happy for you. Lake is a great guy. Paxton wouldn't be friends with him if he wasn't."

"Your brothers are good judges of characters, especially Cal." She nods over at Griffin. "Griffin is a great guy too."

I'm nearly spilling over from trying to keep this secret. I whisper, "Actually, can you keep a secret?"

"Always."

"Something's kind of happened with him."

Willow screams at the top of her lungs, and everyone stops to stare at her. "Sorry," she says with a blush. She grabs my arm, pushing past Brock and Millie who have just shown up to the party. "Tell me all the things," she says as we stand in the laundry room.

"Well." My cheeks flame hot. "I mean…" I can't get the words out.

"Is he a good kisser? Have you had sex?" Her eyes widen. "Oh my god, he's a stallion in the bedroom."

I laugh. "Willow, I can't believe you just asked that."

"Well, is he?"

I nod, my cheeks on fire. "Yes, he's amazing."

Willow clutches her chest. "I'm so happy for you."

"What about Lake?" I ask her when her face falls slightly. "He's good, right?"

Willow sucks in a deep breath, letting it out slowly. "Let's just say, we're still working out the kinks."

I want to ask what this means, but Brock barges into the laundry room. "Mom's looking for you," he says to me, then he stares at Willow. "Should have known you'd be hiding in here from everyone."

"What's that supposed to mean?" Willow crosses her arms against her chest.

"Just means you're probably causing trouble. Getting Anya to do something bad, like when Anya was in high school and you talked her into skipping class."

Willow brushes past me so she can poke a finger into Brock's chest. "That wasn't me, by the way, that was April Billingsworth, and we don't talk to her anymore because she's a mean girl. Just like you're a mean boy."

Brock laughs. "You don't even know me."

"I know you well enough, and you're mean."

Brock steps closer, towering over Willow's shorter frame. "Only to you." And he walks out of the laundry room.

Willow pushes her brown curls off her face. "I hate your brother."

Trying to ease the tension, I laugh. "He's only joking with you, Willow. He isn't only mean to you." But he kind of is.

I don't know what the issue is with Brock and Willow, but they've always fought with each other. Ever since they were little.

Together Willow and I head back into the kitchen, and I smile when I spot Griffin helping my mother cook.

"Did you need me, Mom?" I ask her, and my mother smiles.

"Can you and Griffin head to the store and pick up another jug of milk? We've completely run out."

Willow stifles a laugh beside me, and I nudge her with my elbow. Real smooth.

"Um, sure. Okay." I shake my head, trying my best to pretend my mother isn't the most obvious person in the whole wide world.

Griffin and I walk side by side, heading toward the front door when Callum stops us.

"Where are you two off to?" he asks with an arch of his brow.

"Mom wants us to pick up milk. She says we're out."

"I just saw a full jug in the fridge in the garage." He heads in that direction, and returns quickly with a carton of milk, and Griffin laughs beside me.

Callum hauls Griffin away, and I head back into the kitchen.

"Nice try, Mom," I say.

She shrugs. "Had to try something."

I want to tell my mother all about Griffin and me, but I know my mother, she can *not* keep a secret. And this is a biggie.

"Hi Carol," Millie says, walking into the kitchen with Hartford and Brock.

"Millie, how's the store?" my mother asks her.

Millie's a cute little blonde who owns the local bookstore downtown. She's got these bright blue eyes, and she's always smiling. It shows off her dimples in each cheek.

"It's going well. I can't believe next month will be two years since it's been open."

"Time flies," I say.

"Anya, hey. Claire has been non stop talking about her anniversary dinner you held for her at Atta Boy."

"Yeah, we had a great time."

Tripp stalks into the kitchen, and stops when he sees us all talking.

"Hey Tripp," my mother says. "Did you and Dad figure out the table?"

He shrugs, nods, and flies out of the kitchen like he was just struck by lightning.

"Wonder what his deal is," Brock says, leaning to give Millie a kiss on the cheek. "I'm gonna go and talk to him."

As soon as he leaves I breathe a sigh of relief that the conversation is no longer focused on Griffin and me. I keep wanting to seek him out. Be around him if not only for a second. I wonder if I could text him to meet me up in my bedroom.

No, that's way too risky. But why am I pulling out my phone?

Chapter 20

Griffin

I'm standing outside talking with Callum, Shepherd, Paxton, and Brock. Well, they are talking, my mind is too focused on Anya. Being here with the entire Atwood family is making this secret we have going incredibly difficult. My hands itch to touch her. My lips crave hers. My body is acutely aware of her even when she's not around.

It's hard and I don't just mean the situation.

"Right, Griff?" Callum asks, slapping my back.

"What?" I ask, looking at the four of them.

They all laugh as Paxton shakes his head. "I know that look all too well."

"What look?" Callum asks, staring at me.

"The look of falling in love," Paxton says, smiling.

"What?" Callum and I both ask.

"Who's the girl?" Brock asks.

"Falling in love is a myth," Shepherd says, lifting his shoulders.

"You're dating and didn't tell me?" Callum questions, dipping his brow.

I force a laugh, holding my hands up. "Woah, I don't know what look Pax is talking about, but I'm not in love. Everyone can relax."

Callum visibly calms in front of me as a small grin hits his lips. "I didn't think you'd be with someone without telling me." He wraps his arm around my shoulder and looks at his brothers. "Griffin is like me, more focused on his job than anything else."

I'm an asshole. I'm a complete and total asshole.

"Is it sex? Are you having great sex? Cause that look doesn't lie," Paxton pushes.

"Griffin isn't a liar, why the hell would he start now?" Callum says, rushing to my defense.

Only I am a liar and I don't intend to stop. I'm not in love like Paxton thinks, at least I don't think I am. I might be. Actually, scratch that, I think I am. All I know is, I'm having the best sex of my life—with their sister. Breaking promises and lying to everyone is fucked up, but I can't stop.

"Hey, I heard about the big party Atta Boy will be hosting," Don says, interrupting our conversation. I've never been more grateful in my life.

"Yeah, it's huge. There's going to be an article in the paper about it," Callum says, smiling.

"I'm incredibly proud of you all, especially Anya. She's really taken to this and proven to be a huge asset," Don continues.

They all start talking about the party and I feel my phone buzz in my pocket. I pull it out and my heart slams against my chest when I see it's Anya.

> Anya: Feeling risky?

> With you...always.

> Anya: Meet me in my room ;)

> Careful baby, you're playing a dangerous game here.

> Anya: My panties are sliding down my legs.

"Going to the bathroom, be right back," I say, rushing inside.

I glance around and see Carol busy in the kitchen with Hartford, Willow, and Millie. Lake is standing off to the side trying to talk to Tripp who looks like he'd rather be anywhere else.

No one notices me and I quickly make my way to the stairs, taking them two at a time. Her bedroom door is half closed and I push it open, standing in the doorway.

"Teasing me in front of everyone is a bad idea," I say, stepping inside and quietly closing the door behind me. I keep my eyes locked on her mischievous eyes as I press the lock on the door. "Lift your dress." She does as I demand and she in fact has no panties on. "Fuck," I hiss, racing toward her.

I slam my lips to hers as my fingers sink into her bare ass. She moans as I push my hard cock against her. Her nails dig into my shoulders as I deepen the kiss, needing her more in this moment than I need the next breath I take.

My one hand moves to her pussy and I drag my fingers through her wetness. I use my other hand to unbutton my jeans and with a little work, push them past my ass. My dick rubs against her and she moans a little too loudly.

I break the kiss and search her heated eyes. "You can't make noise, Anya. They'll all come rushing."

She bites her lip to hide her smile, but nods her head. "It's dangerous and I like it a little too much."

"You want danger?"

Her eyes bounce between mine as a small grin takes over my lips. I reach down and pull her sundress off, tossing it behind me. She's now completely exposed to me, but it's not enough. I kick off my jeans and boxers, lifting her into my arms in one quick motion. I kiss her neck as I walk toward the window in her bedroom. "Your family is outside, better hope they don't look up and see," I whisper, pressing her naked body to the window.

"Griffin," she whisper-shouts with wide eyes.

I slam into her and her mouth falls open as her fingers dig into my upper arms. "You want danger, and I warned you not to tease me."

I pound into her hard and fast, her hard nipples easily felt through the thin fabric of my shirt. Her dripping wet pussy grips me tightly as I continue my punishing rhythm.

"Oh God, Griffin," she moans.

"Shh, I told you not to make any noise," I warn.

My fingers dig harder into her ass as her head falls forward onto my shoulder. She bites it lightly to keep from screaming and it's fucking hot.

I know I need to make this fast because someone will notice us missing, and as exciting and dangerous as this is, I don't want to actually get caught.

"Reach down and rub your clit, Anya. I need to feel you come," I hiss.

She doesn't hesitate and does exactly what I ask. Her teeth sink harder into my shoulder and it only spurs me on. I drive into her harder and faster, ensuring we aren't rattling the window.

"I'm so close," she whispers, going right back to biting my shoulder.

"Good girl, come for me. Give me your release because I promise you it is only the appetizer to what I have in store for you when we get the fuck out of here."

Her body reacts and her pussy grips me like a vice. Her teeth quite possibly have broken skin as her muffled cries surround us.

Her release continues and pulls mine from me just as quickly. We both hold on tightly to each other as we breathe heavily.

I press a soft kiss to her neck and she lifts her head. Our eyes lock and I grin, walking us away from the window.

"Wow, that was, holy wow," she whispers.

I chuckle as I place her back onto her feet. "That's dangerous and careless, but now maybe we can get through this dinner without bursting into flames."

"Anya?" Carol shouts up the stairs.

"Shit," she says, rushing around to get dressed.

As I slip my jeans back on, I grab her panicked face and smile. "Relax, baby. I'm going to go out first and slip into the bathroom. You're going to fix yourself up very quickly and go downstairs. You'll tell everyone that you were on the phone with the Mayor giving him details about the dinner choices. They'll be so excited about that, that when I enter they won't question anything." I kiss her soft lips and rest my forehead to hers. "I'm not going to let anyone be none the wiser."

She nods still looking nervous as I poke my head out of her room and slip into the bathroom. I listen carefully for her and when I hear her walk down the stairs, I wait five minutes.

That was much needed and I feel like I can finally relax around everyone. It also makes me wonder if what Paxton said is true. Am I in love with Anya?

I kind of always think I have been. Just too afraid to ever admit it.

⊏⊐

"Dinner is delicious, Mom," Brock says, savoring a mouthful of roast chicken.

"Yes, everything is amazing," Callum agrees, nodding enthusiastically as he reaches for another helping of mashed potatoes.

No one questioned me after I appeared shortly after Anya. They were all so excited about her fake phone call that they didn't notice my delayed arrival. The dinner table is buzzing with conversation and laughter, the clinking of cutlery punctuating the cheerful atmosphere. It's a reminder of how fortunate I am to share such a close bond with everyone here.

My eyes keep finding Anya's across the table, and each time they do, my heart beats faster in my chest. Her presence stirs emotions in me that I never knew existed, feelings that are becoming irresistibly addictive.

"Mom and I made some chocolates to go with the apple pie for dessert," Anya says, her smile lighting up the room as her eyes meet mine.

"I keep telling her she should offer her treats more often for parties. They are always delicious," I add, holding her gaze, a silent connection passing between us.

"That's not a bad idea. If anyone knows food, it's Griffin," Callum says, gesturing toward me with his fork.

"Hey," Carol says with a laugh, giving Callum a playful nudge.

"Of course, you too, Mom," Callum quickly adds, his face breaking into a grin as everyone chuckles.

Everyone laughs as Paxton stands up, raising his glass. "Dinner has been perfect, Mom. Thank you. And Dad, thanks for setting everything up." We all chuckle at his gratitude, sharing a warm moment of appreciation for our parents.

Paxton takes a deep breath, his smile widening. "I asked Mom and Dad if they could host this dinner because Hartford and I have an announcement."

The room falls silent, everyone at the table leaning in slightly, anticipation hanging in the air. We all have our suspicions, but we're finally about to hear it from Paxton himself.

"Hartford has been my best friend since kindergarten, and I've loved her every day since the day I first met her. Best friends, boyfriend and girlfriend. Last night, I asked her if she would like to add wife to that description, and she said yes. Hartford and I are getting married."

The room erupts in joyful noise. Carol, overcome with emotion, wipes her tears as she jumps up to hug the newly engaged couple. Everyone is offering their congratulations, voices overlapping in a chorus of happiness and excitement.

Amidst the celebration, my eyes find Anya's. She's watching with tears glistening in her eyes, a radiant smile on her face. The love she has for Paxton and Hartford is palpable, reflected in her teary gaze.

Under the table, I reach out and find her knee, giving it a gentle squeeze. Her eyes meet mine, and she smiles, a look that takes my breath away. My heart races as I return her smile, feeling a rush of emotions.

We both glance back at Paxton and Hartford, who are locked in an adoring gaze, their smiles brighter than ever. The love between them is unmistakable, a testament to their journey together.

Holy shit.

My eyes drift back to Anya, and in that moment, everything becomes clear.

Paxton is right—I am in love.

The realization hits me like a tidal wave, profound and undeniable. Anya's presence, her smile, the way she makes me feel —it all points to one truth. I'm in love, and it's the most incredible feeling in the world.

Chapter 21

Anya

I can't believe my older brother is getting married. And to Hartford of all people. I love Hartford. She's like a sister to me —we've practically grown up together. My heart swells with joy and disbelief.

Unable to contain my emotion any longer, I rise from the table and envelop Hartford in a warm hug. The rest of the family follows suit, standing up and surrounding Paxton and Hartford with congratulatory embraces.

"I can't believe you'll finally be my sister," I tell Hartford, my voice thick with happiness.

"Let's celebrate!" my father announces, popping the cork off a bottle of champagne with a satisfying pop. "I'm so happy to welcome Hartford to the family."

My mother winks at Hartford. "I always knew she'd be my daughter someday."

"Wow," Callum says, the only one still seated. His face is a picture of astonishment, clearly gobsmacked by the news.

I pat his shoulder, teasingly. "What's wrong? Did you think since you're the oldest you'd get married first?"

Callum shakes his head slowly, a bemused smile playing on his lips. "I've never even once thought about marriage. For me, or for any of you."

"Well, obviously it's bound to happen," I say, my eyes shifting to Griffin, who is standing across from me. A smile tugs at my lips as I imagine a future with him, just like Paxton and Hartford. With my family.

Griffin has been a staple in our household, just like Hartford. The thought strikes me suddenly, and I can't believe I'm about to think this, but I'd marry him if he ever asked. I shake my head at my own silly thoughts. He'd never ask me. I'm sure this is just something fun for him. He's not serious.

However, the way he's looking at me right now, with an intensity that makes my heart skip a beat, makes me nearly hyperventilate. His gaze is so earnest, so full of emotion, it feels like he could get down on one knee at any moment.

My breath catches in my throat as the possibility lingers between us, making the room spin with the heady mix of celebration and unspoken feelings.

"Are you okay?" Millie asks me, concern etched on her face.

I turn to face her, taking in her light-blonde hair and bright blue eyes. She's really very pretty, and I'm genuinely happy that Brock is dating her. I nod. "I'm fine. It's just a lot to take in."

Millie's smile lights up her face. "I was kind of expecting it, honestly. Those two are made for each other."

"Like you and Brock?" I tease, giving her a playful wink.

Her expression shifts, her smile faltering. "Umm, we're not that serious."

Sensing I've touched on a sensitive topic, I quickly change the subject. "Look at how happy my mother is," I say, gesturing towards Mom, who is practically glowing with joy.

"She does look happy. So do Paxton and Hartford."

"Yeah, I guess I shouldn't be so shocked. I just thought they would date forever."

Millie laughs, and Tripp steps closer, joining our conversation. "I can't wait to go to their wedding."

"Weddings suck," Tripp mutters, not looking particularly thrilled for the couple.

The whole room starts returning to their seats, but Millie stares at Tripp as if he's just said the worst thing imaginable. "When the couple is as in love as Hartford and Paxton are, the wedding is amazing."

Tripp gazes at Millie, his expression softening. "I am happy for them, you know?" He runs a hand through his hair, looking a bit awkward. "I'm not a complete jerk."

Millie touches his arm gently. "I didn't think you were."

Tripp glances down at where Millie's hand rests on his arm, then pulls back. "I need to finish my meal," he says hurriedly, retreating to his seat.

I smile at Millie as she resumes her seat next to Brock, who is beaming with pride and happiness.

"When's the date?" my mother asks, her excitement palpable.

Paxton laughs, his eyes sparkling. "I just asked her, Mom."

Everyone chuckles, the room filling with a warm, affectionate atmosphere. The clinking of champagne glasses and murmured congratulations add to the celebratory mood. My eyes wander to Willow, who is chatting animatedly with Hartford, her face glowing with happiness. I can't help but think about how perfect everything feels in this moment.

As we all settle back down, I catch Griffin's eye again. The way he's looking at me, so full of warmth and something deeper, makes my heart race. Maybe, just maybe, there's a future for us too. A future as bright and full of love as the one Paxton and Hartford are stepping into.

"How many people?" Callum asks, his tone brisk and businesslike.

"Thirty-five. Nothing too crazy," I say, glancing up from my computer screen. I'm typing up the Banquet Event Order (BEO) for the upcoming function with the Mayor. Callum is breathing down my neck about the details, while Griffin sits in the corner of my office, a thoughtful smile on his face.

"I'm thinking we should do something different for this party. Something that sets us apart," Griffin says, catching our attention.

"Like what?" Callum asks, his curiosity piqued.

"We need to have the best for them. Top-of-the-line menu, top-of-the-line drink choices. You all should create a signature drink just for them. Or maybe name one of the beers after them— something you haven't released yet. Just for the party," Griffin suggests, standing from his seat and pacing the room as he speaks. "Something that shows we go above and beyond for our guests."

"I love that," I say, beaming at the idea.

Callum nods in agreement. "Me too. I'm going to get with Shepherd and Brock on developing something special. Brock just developed a new coffee porter—we can name it for the party."

"Yes, I love that idea. They're all a bunch of office workers, so we can play with the coffee and work theme." I shake my head, thinking. "Or we can gear it toward the travel destination aspect of Atta Boy."

Griffin points at me, his eyes lighting up. "Yes. Great idea. The Perfect Porter. Or something that encapsulates everything Atta Boy stands for."

Callum agrees. "I'll see what the guys say." He leaves the office, heading off to brainstorm with Shepherd and Brock.

I turn back to Griffin, who is now looking at me with a different kind of intensity. His eyes have gone from excited to something much deeper, and it sends a thrill through me.

"You know," I say, stepping closer to him, "your idea really could set us apart."

Griffin smiles, closing the distance between us. "I'm glad you think so. We need to always be thinking ahead, staying innovative."

"Absolutely," I reply, feeling the electricity between us.

He wraps an arm around me, peering over his shoulder to make sure the office door is closed. "I need you, Anya."

My eyes widen. "We can *not* do it in here," my voice trails off, and I quickly add, "again."

"I can't stop thinking about you. Stay at my place tonight." He tugs on me, bringing me closer. "Please. Don't make me beg."

I raise a brow. "I kind of like it when you beg," I say with a light laugh.

He brushes his mouth against my ear, causing a cascade of shivers to race down my spine. "I'll beg you all night long. I'll beg you to spread those long, luscious legs of yours so I can eat your pussy. I'll beg you to suck me off with that magic mouth of yours."

I'm so turned on. "I will," I say, letting him know I'm game for all of it. Staying the night. Spreading my legs. Hell, I may kneel right here and right now to watch him get off while I suck his dick.

I love watching the faces he makes when I suck him. It's like he can't get enough of me. Like he's never been so turned on in his life.

His phone vibrates in his pocket, and he pulls away. He reaches for his phone out of his chef's jacket pocket. "It's Tripp. I told him to come find me when he gets to work today."

"Yeah. We shouldn't be doing this here at work." I smile at him. "I'll stay over tonight."

He breathes a sigh of relief. "I can't wait." And then he heads out of my office door, and I sink back into my office chair.

I'm becoming so addicted to this man. I really can't keep my feelings for him hidden much longer.

Chapter 22

Griffin

I contemplate the menu for the Mayor's party as I flip the burgers that have been ordered for lunch. Tripp walks back into the kitchen with that sour puss look on his face that seems to be permanent these days.

"Just waiting on those burgers," he says, leaning against the counter and pulling out his phone.

"Tripp," I say, holding up my spatula. "I've given you time. I've yelled. I've worked you to the bone. I've tried talking to you. I've kept your secret of being arrested. Yet, you're still moping around, stuck in your head. It's time man, tell me what the hell is going on with you."

He sighs and pushes his phone back into his pocket. He glances at me and I see sadness or maybe hurt in his eyes. "Can I ask you a question?"

I quickly get the burgers off, placing them on the buns. "Please, I wish you would."

"Have you ever liked someone and at first you felt like they had no idea you existed and then you realize there's something huge standing in the way and you know your luck has run out?"

I stare at him, wondering if he's talking about me and Anya or about himself. I clear my throat and wipe my now sweaty hands on my apron. "Are you saying you like a girl?" I ask, hoping it's this direction he's going in.

"Yeah," he whispers.

Relief washes over me knowing my secret is still hidden. It's fucked up because part of the reason I need Anya at my place tonight is to confess my feelings and yet, I still can't bring myself to reveal this relationship to Callum or any of the Atwoods. I refuse to let her go and I have no idea how it's all going to work out. The only thing I know for sure is that my life is better with Anya in it.

"So, no advice?" Tripp asks, pulling me back to the conversation.

"What's standing in the way?"

He shrugs, looking down at the floor. "Can't say."

"All right, listen. You want to get this girl's attention right?" He peeks up at me and nods. "Tripp, girls want men who are confident in themselves and their choices. You running around with the wrong crowd, getting drunk, and being arrested, that's not a turn-on for anyone. If you want to get her attention, you need to show her you're worth that attention." I grab his shoulder and smile at him. "Work hard in school, bust your ass at the brewery. Allow her to see you have goals and ambitions. Whatever is standing in the way, it won't matter if it's meant to be. If you show her the guy that I know you are, she'll not only notice you, she'll be all in. Your luck hasn't run out. You're just starting out in life, there's nothing that can stand in your way."

He shoves his hands in his pockets and looks at the ground before lifting his eyes to me. "You really think that will work?"

"You really like this girl, huh?"

"Yeah, I do," he whispers.

"It'll work, Tripp, believe me. And a little flirting never hurt either."

He chuckles at that and nods.

I should've known it was a girl problem. We've all been there. Every guy loses his shit over a girl at some point. Although, as I think about it, I never have. I've never gotten close enough to anyone to allow it to affect me in any way. I never fought over a girl. I never got drunk over a girl. I never went out looking for a rebound.

I guess it doesn't happen to every guy or maybe it doesn't happen until you've found the right girl.

That thought makes me realize, if Anya walked away, I would, in fact, lose my shit.

I focus back on Tripp because it's much easier than allowing myself to get into my head.

"Tripp, everyone at some point feels like they need to fight for the right person. You aren't alone. Just know that."

He smirks and stands a little taller. "You fighting for someone?"

I grin and turn my back to him. "Get these burgers out before they get cold."

"Seriously? I just poured my heart out to you," he says.

"It's called a private life for a reason. Now, please get these burgers out."

I wish I could go out to the bar, jump on top of it and tell everyone about Anya. I wish I could kiss her without hiding. I wish I didn't carry this guilt of lying to everyone. Anya included. She deserves better. I just don't know how to approach the subject of telling everyone.

⊏⊐

After a long day at work, all I can think about on my drive home is being with Anya. There's so much to be said, but I can't focus on any of it until I have her.

She pulls in the driveway behind me and I lift her over my shoulder when she gets out of the car.

"Woah," she says with a laugh.

"I need to get you inside fast," I say, unlocking the door quickly before pushing it open.

I slam the door closed behind us and carry her straight to my bedroom. Once inside, I allow her to slide down my body. Her arms wrap around my neck and I pull her to me, pressing my lips to hers. A soft moan escapes her and I sink my fingers into her hair, breaking the kiss.

"I did nothing but think of you all day. I need you, baby." I kiss her again and tighten my hold on her hair. "Now."

I reach down and quickly pull up the gray skirt she's wearing and hook my fingers into her panties, pushing them down her legs. As they fall, I get my jeans and boxers down past my knees. I lift her into my arms and she wraps her legs around me as I spin around and push her back against the wall.

My hard cock presses against her and she moans, locking her heated eyes with mine. "Fuck me, Griffin."

I slam into her and her head falls back, smacking into the wall as her fingers dig into my shoulders. I move my hands to hold onto her round ass as I continue to pound into her.

"Watching you from afar all day is driving me fucking crazy," I hiss.

She groans her understanding as my fingers dig into her ass as I drive into her harder and faster.

"Oh Griffin, I'm not going to last," she cries out.

"Me either, baby. You've had me hard all day," I grunt out.

Her cries of pleasure spur me on as I fight to keep my release from crashing over me.

"I'm so close."

"Rub your clit, baby. Reach between us and come on me."

Her hand slips between us and she rubs her clit, crying out. I feel her tighten around me and I close my eyes lost in the feelings she's awakened in me.

"Oh God, Griffin," she screams as her release crashes over her.

"Fuck, that's it, baby. Come all over me."

She's still shaking from her orgasm when I find mine. "Anya," I whisper, leaning forward and burying my face in her neck.

Her hands move up my body and she pushes them into my hair. "You all right?" she whispers.

I nod against her, still breathing heavily. I press a soft kiss to her neck and lift my head. "Better than I've ever been."

We clean up and adjust our clothes, laughing about how we didn't even manage to get them off. That's what she does to me. The need is so great that I can't even wait to get her naked.

Once we're done, I grab her hand and nod my head. "I want to talk to you."

I lead her out into the living room and we both sit on the couch. She turns to face me and I rest my elbows on my knees.

She rubs my back, moving closer. "Talk to me, Griffin. I can sense something is wrong."

"Nothing is wrong," I say, turning my head to look at her. "Did you ever wonder why I spent so much time at your house growing up?"

"At the time, no, but it's been something I took closer notice to recently."

She keeps lightly rubbing my back and it gives me a feeling of comfort that I need. "My childhood was not good. My father was and still is a cheater, only now he's also a drunk. He didn't like noise, he didn't like mess, he didn't like me. My mother never stood up for me, never stood up for herself. I was scared and lonely. When I met Callum, he didn't ask what it was like at home, he just knew I needed a friend. He'd invite me over and my mother was all too happy to get me out of the house. No mess or noise for her cheating husband to come home to."

I see the tears swimming in her eyes and I don't like that she's feeling what I went through, but I can't stop now. I've never told anyone but Callum and it's time I let her fully in.

"When I was at your house I felt a sense of belonging and freedom. I could laugh and play and be a kid. I loved being there, but I always had to go home. When I was a kid I would just slip into my room and be as quiet as I could. Especially after my father threw away my favorite toy cars because he found one in the living room. It was devastating and I tried to make sure that didn't happen again."

"Oh Griffin, I'm so sorry," she interrupts.

I force a grin and shrug. "The older I got the harder it got to be the little boy who sat hidden in my room. My father and I fought a lot. My mother and I fought a lot. Every time I tried to defend her, she would get angry with me. I couldn't understand but I guess it's just something I'm not meant to understand. My father never changed his ways and the moment I could get out of that house, I ran. If it wasn't for your family, for your brother, I honestly don't know what would've happened to me."

She wraps her arms around me, resting her head on my shoulder. "I had no idea it was so awful for you. I'm sorry."

"I don't like talking about it, so only Callum and now you know. When I think about it, it stirs an anger inside me that I don't like." I turn my head to see her the best I can. "Until I met you."

She sits up and searches my face. "What?"

"Until I met you that anger would bubble up inside me and I'd lash out, but you calm it, Anya. I didn't think it was possible for me to feel things like a normal person. It's not like I was shown love and I wasn't even sure it was something that existed. I saw it with your family, but my blood is made up of something else entirely. And until you, I was fine with one night stands and dead end relationships."

I turn and pull her onto my lap, tucking a piece of hair behind her ear as I stare at her gorgeous face. "I didn't think I'd ever love someone or be the kind of guy that could be loved. Yet, here I am." I press a soft kiss to her full lips and smile. "I love you, Anya Atwood."

Tears swim in her eyes as she smiles down at me. "I wasn't sure if this was more for you or if it was just all in fun. I've tried fighting my feelings, pushing them aside, but I saw glimpses of your feelings and started allowing myself to feel mine." She presses a kiss to my lips and rests her forehead against mine. "You are so full of love and worth being loved. I love you too, Griffin Cole."

I close my eyes and allow her words to sink in. She loves me.

It's the first time I've ever said these words and the first time anyone has ever said them to me.

I'm going to have to talk to Callum because Anya is mine.

It's time everyone knows.

Chapter 23

Anya

It's been a few days since Griffin and I confessed our love for one another, and yet, we're still hiding our relationship. I honestly don't understand why.

Every time I try to bring it up, something happens, and another day passes where we keep our relationship a secret.

I head downstairs on the day of the Mayor's party, and my mother's in the kitchen. "Hey Mom, I'm heading to the brewery to set up for tonight."

"I put all your chocolates in a box. I can't wait for the committee to see how much work you've put into everything."

I nod. "I just hope everything goes smoothly tonight."

My mother's warm smile gives me comfort. "It will."

I hug my mother, thinking about what Griffin said about his own family. I couldn't imagine growing up that way, and the thought of it makes me love Griffin even more.

"You look happy," my mother says, and I laugh.

"I am happy."

"Wouldn't be a six-foot-two young man making you happy, now is it?"

My eyes widen. "No," I say, but it's totally a lie.

"Anya, I know you haven't been sleeping here at night. I'm not going to pretend you're staying with Willow every night."

I cover my mouth as a huge smile splits my face. "I am staying with Willow."

My mother places her hands on my shoulders. "I'm not stupid."

I drop my hands. "I know, it's just we're trying to keep it a secret."

"Secrets have a way of making themselves known."

I nod. "I know. Honestly, I don't even know why we're waiting."

My mother steps away to grab the box of chocolates. "I would suspect it isn't easy for Griffin to come clean with your brothers. But I'm sure they'll see how much Griffin cares about you. I think he always has. I remember when you came home once for college and Griffin was here. The way he stared at you." My mother clutches her chest. "I'll never forget it."

"Really?" How come I've never noticed?

"I think he's always had a thing for you."

Goosebumps cascade all down my arms. "I wish I'd have known."

My mother's smile is wide. "No, it's much better this way. You both are finally in a position to be able to give each other the things you both need."

"Did you know about his home life?" I ask my mother. "When he was growing up?"

"Callum once told me it wasn't good there. I've only seen his mother in passing. The grocery store. The shopping centers. I've only seen his father once, and he scared me."

"He did? Why?"

"He's not a nice man. He was drunk, causing a raucous at the high school once. Griffin and Callum had gotten into a fight with a few of the other kids, and his father was so angry. We didn't see Griffin for a few weeks after that."

Chills skate over me. "I love him, Mom."

My mother wraps her arms around me. "Good. He needs a woman like you."

"Like me?"

"Yes, a good woman who understands him. Who can love him for who he is."

I think about my mother's words, and it makes my heart beat in my chest harder for Griffin. "He said he loves me too."

My mother's eyes beam at me. "Good. I think you two are perfect for each other. Sometimes I feel like I know who my children are going to end up with, and I always knew you two would end up together."

I laugh, swatting my mother's arm playfully. "That's not true."

"It is. I knew Paxton and Hartford would end up together."

I laugh harder. "We all knew that."

"I know you and Griffin will end up together."

"What about Callum? Is he ever going to meet anyone?" I can't possibly imagine my oldest brother falling in love.

My mother sighs. "I honestly don't know about him. Whoever he does get with will need to have the patience of a saint."

"What about Brock and Millie? I think they're cute together."

My mother shakes her head. "No, Brock needs a challenge, and Millie needs somebody who can appreciate her." My mother winks at me, and I glance at the clock on the oven.

"Oh shoot, I need to get going." I give my mother another quick hug, and grab the box of chocolates to make my way to the brewery.

Make sure the tables are set up perfectly.

Tripp: Or what?

Griffin: Don't be an ass, Tripp.

Tonight is so important for the future of the brewery. I can't play around.

Callum: Agreed. And don't worry, I'm personally making sure everything is up to par.

Thank you. I'll be there in fifteen minutes.

Griffin: Can't wait.

I glance down at the group chat, rereading Griffin's text for the fifth time. Did he really mean for everyone to read that? The chat went silent as soon as his message delivered, and now I can't help but wonder if everyone is thinking it's weird. Is it just me overanalyzing, or did Griffin just drop a bombshell?

I hate that my mind is overthinking every single thing. What are my brothers thinking right now? The uncertainty is driving me crazy.

But at the same time, I feel this overwhelming urge to tell everyone about us. Why should we hide our relationship? I understand how hard it must be for Griffin to tell my brothers, but at the same time, I don't see them caring whether we're dating or not. They've always wanted me to be happy, right?

It's none of their business, I remind myself. It's nobody's business but our own. Yet, a small voice inside me whispers that maybe, just maybe, sharing this part of my life could bring us all closer. Or, it could complicate everything.

I shake the feelings away and try to focus on the task at hand —the party.

I pull up to the brewery with tons of time to spare. We're going to pull this party off without a hitch. The local paper ran a story yesterday, calling our brewery as a 'new up and coming hang out spot' and it did an expose on Callum and Griffin. It said Griffin, and I quote, 'was a master in the kitchen.'

I'm so proud of him, and my mother is talking about getting the article framed. She wants to hang it up in the dining room.

I rush inside the brewery, dropping off the box of chocolates in the party room before I head around to say my hellos. Not that I even have time for that, but I can't deny the fact that I'm bursting at the seams to see Griffin.

When I step into the kitchen he's having a quick meeting with the other chefs.

"I want tonight to go smoothly. If you need anything you make sure I know about it before it becomes a problem. We've got everything prepped, so I don't see running out of things a problem."

The other chefs nod, and Griffin smiles at me when I step up closer.

"Remember, if Anya needs anything you make sure the party is top priority," he says, dismissing them afterward.

"How's it going?" I ask him.

"We're good to go for tonight."

I smile, wanting desperately to mention the text. To talk about everything that's going on between us. "I need to print out the menus in my office."

"I'll come with you," Griffin says, following me out of the kitchen.

It's not unusual to have him come with me to print out the menus, so nobody even questions us as we walk into my office. I fire up my computer, starting the printing job and then I lean back in my chair as Griffin stands over me.

"I've missed the fuck out of you," he says, knowing nobody can hear him except me.

"My mother knows about us," I tell him, more so to gauge his reaction to the news.

The look of surprise on his face is unexpected. He almost appears afraid. "She's not going to tell anyone, is she?"

I stand from my chair, crossing my arms. "Would it be so awful if she did?"

Griffin's eyes search mine, a mix of worry and confusion. He steps away from me, plunging a hand into his dark locks. "Um, yes, Anya. I'm not ready to tell anyone just yet."

I park a hand on my hip, frustration bubbling up. "And when will you be ready? Once I pop out a few kids? Will you be ready then?"

He steps closer, his eyes blazing into mine. "No, I just…I don't know. I want to tell everyone…" His words trail off when there's a knock on my office door.

I open it to find Tripp standing there. "There you are," he says, walking into my office. "Callum sent me here to find the tablecloths. Do you know where they are?"

I let out a frustrated breath, trying to push down the turmoil roiling inside me. "Yeah, they're in this box." I move to the shelf behind my desk, pulling out a big box of tablecloths. "Here."

"Did I interrupt something?" Tripp asks, his eyes volleying back and forth between Griffin and me.

"No, it's fine," Griffin says, his voice tight as he leaves my office. I'm left standing there, even more confused than I was before. Why the secrecy?

I help Tripp with the tablecloths, trying to focus on the task at hand. Before long, the party room transforms from ordinary to spectacular, with vibrant colors and elegant decorations. Despite the beauty of the room, my mind is still spinning with questions.

Why is Griffin so afraid to let others know about us? What is he so worried about? As I arrange the last tablecloth, I can't shake the feeling that this secrecy might be a sign of deeper issues. And I wonder, how long can we keep hiding before it all comes crashing down?

Chapter 24

Griffin

I feel as if there's a weight on my shoulders that is currently getting heavy to bear. As I swiftly walk toward the kitchen, everything that just happened in Anya's office plays in a loop in my mind.

"My mother knows about us?"

"When will you be ready? When I pop out a few kids?"

I feel a drop of sweat trickle down my back as I push into the kitchen. The secret we've been keeping is slowly coming to the surface and I'm not ready for the fallout of it.

I broke a promise I made to Callum and I see no way of making him understand I had no choice. He doesn't understand love. He will cut me out as his friend and the likelihood that I lose my job is pretty damn high. I never wanted to choose between Anya and Callum, but I'm afraid that's the direction we're headed.

Carol knows and it's only a matter of time before Don is told. I have no idea how he'll react to the news. Will he accept our relationship or will he deem me damaged goods?

There are so many ways this could blow up in my face and I'm terrified that in the end, I'll be the one left standing alone.

"Chef, the article in the paper about you was impressive. Congratulations."

I nod to Charles, one of my sous chefs. "Thanks," I mumble.

Of course, I read the article. Being described as a master in the kitchen had me smiling like a damn fool. It's a compliment that truly made me proud.

I've overcome a lot in my life, mainly my father, and although only two people know how horrible it was, I feel like I've accomplished things that seemed unreachable. I didn't think I'd survive childhood, let alone get a culinary degree. I never would've imagined being the head chef at any restaurant, never mind being a co-owner with my best friends. I sure as hell didn't think I'd ever experience love and yet here I am, desperately in love with Anya.

None of it was handed to me. I've busted my ass for everything. Christ, I had to chase after Anya to give me a chance.

Now just when I feel like I have everything that I could possibly ever want, I could lose it all.

I close my eyes briefly and take a deep breath. "No, fuck that," I whisper to myself. I've fought for everything I have and I'm not going to stop now. I don't know how I'll do it, but I'm determined to have it all.

"Hey, the room is set up and Anya is kinda in bitch mode, so watch out," Tripp says, grinning as he walks into the kitchen.

"Hey, don't talk about your sister that way."

"You know, someone recently told me that every guy fights for the right woman," he says, grabbing a stack of napkins.

"Sounds like a smart guy," I say, chuckling.

"He is if he takes his own advice," he says, walking out of the kitchen.

For fuck's sake.

"Griff, you sure everything is good for tonight," Callum asks, rushing into the kitchen.

I know tonight is a big deal, but he's been over the top the last few days. Now that I have the worry of my secret being exposed, I'm feeling that fire inside me that Anya has been so good at keeping at bay.

"Yeah, Callum, I told you a hundred times. I've got everything handled. It will be a perfectly executed dinner. Fucking relax."

Yep, I regret the words as they slip out of my mouth.

"What the hell did you just say? You want me to fucking relax when we have the potential for the biggest thing to happen at the brewery? You want me to fucking relax and let it all fall to shit and let our—mine and yours—reputation be disgraced? Maybe you shouldn't be so relaxed like you've been the last few weeks. I've noticed how different you've been and I wasn't going to say anything, but seriously what the hell is going on?"

I blow out a breath as I try to compose myself. "I didn't mean it. You know me better than that. I just meant try not to stress yourself out so much. I promise you that everything is handled in this kitchen. I would never disappoint you or this brewery. Give me a little credit. I'm sorry it came out the way it did," I say, hoping to deflect from his last bit of questioning.

He sighs and leans against the counter, scrubbing his face. "I didn't mean to bite your head off. I just want this to go perfectly. I want us all to have the success that we deserve."

I grab his shoulder and nod. "We already have success, don't forget that. This party is monumental, I'm not denying that, but don't dismiss what we've accomplished already. You allow the world to fall on your shoulders, but Cal, we're all in this together. We all know exactly what needs to be done to show the Mayor and his guests that we truly are the fucking best. Trust in that."

He smiles, shaking his head. "You might be a master in the kitchen, but you're also a genius with words. Thanks, man."

After our talk, Callum leaves and hopefully has relaxed a little. I continue to stay busy in the kitchen, making sure I don't disappoint anyone tonight. I haven't seen Anya since I walked out of her office and damn I miss her already.

The party is in full swing and it is going as perfectly as Callum and Anya hoped for. The food has been served and my job is over, but I won't leave. Just like every party I'll be here long after closing with Anya.

I decided to step out of the kitchen and watch from afar. I've been watching Callum talking and laughing with all the big wigs in the room. He fits in perfectly with them. I've been watching Tripp bust his ass to stay on top of everything and it makes me smile thinking he's taking my advice. I watched Brock and Shepherd serve the new beer and the looks of amazement on everyone's face that tasted it.

But what I've really been focused on is Anya. The way she flawlessly carries herself as the professional woman she is.

How she interacts with each person is different and it's mesmerizing to watch. The way her face lights up when she's given a compliment or the sound of her laughter escaping the room. The way she lights up the room just by stepping into it. She's breathtaking and I find myself leaning against the wall to keep from falling to my knees.

She's now talking to the Mayor with a huge smile on her face that has my heart racing. I pull out my phone and grin.

> Damn baby, you look almost as sexy talking to the Mayor as you do naked in my bed.

I smile as I hit send and glance up to watch her reaction. She rests her hand on her pocket and I know she felt her phone vibrate. I peek down at my phone and my smile slips.

"No, no, no. Fuck no," I whisper, staring at the text.

I didn't send it to just Anya, I sent it to the group text. *With everyone.* I still had it pulled up from earlier and accidentally sent it through to that.

"Fuck," I whisper, running my hand through my hair.

I glance around as my heart feels like it's going to burst out of my chest. Tripp catches my eye and laughs. Fuck. Brock looks at his phone and his brow dips. Shepherd left after serving the beer.

Just as I turn to make a run for it, Callum comes out of his office, pulling his phone from his pocket.

"Fuck," I whisper.

He reads the text and looks at me before glancing over at the Mayor. It takes him all of three seconds to put it all together before he's rushing toward me.

"You son of a bitch," he shouts.

He goes to take a swing, but I grab his arm and shake my head. "Please, not here. Everyone at the party will see and it will ruin our reputation."

He gives a humorless laugh as his eyes narrow. "You think I give a fuck about your reputation when you've been fucking my sister. My sister, Griffin. You broke a promise, you son of a bitch. You're lucky I don't kill you right now," he shouts.

Anya glances over when she hears the commotion and excuses herself from the Mayor.

"Callum, let me explain," I rush out.

He grabs onto my chef's coat, pulling me closer to his face. "You're a fucking liar. I don't want to hear shit you have to say. You stay away from me and my sister. I'm not asking you, I'm fucking telling you. If I so much as see you look in her direction, I will fucking kill you."

"Callum, stop it," Anya says, trying to pull him off me and push us out of the room.

"Anya, don't," I plead.

"Don't fucking talk to her," he hisses.

Brock and Tripp rush over at this point. I'm humiliated at the scene that is being caused.

"Callum, what the hell, let go of him," Brock says, trying to get between us.

"Brock, I deserve it," I say.

"What?" Anya says. "This is why you wanted to keep us a secret because you knew Callum was going to act like an animal?"

Callum snaps his angry green eyes toward her. "He wanted you to keep it a secret because he broke a promise. A promise that he swore he'd never break. When I told him to promise he'd never touch my little sister."

"What? You made him promise not to touch me?" she shouts. Her sad eyes slide to mine and the hurt I see shatters my heart. "You were never going to tell anyone, were you? I was a dirty little secret that you intended to keep hidden."

"Callum, seriously?" Brock says.

"Now it's making sense," Tripp whispers with a sly smile.

"Well, look at the prodigal son," a booming voice says from the middle of the room, causing all eyes to look over.

Callum lets go of me and I feel like the wind has been knocked out of me.

My father. In the flesh. And he's here.

Why?

"Dad, what the hell?"

I haven't seen or spoken to him in nearly four years and tonight, while my world is falling apart, he chooses to make a fucking appearance.

"I saw you in the paper," he says, holding up the article. "Seems my boy is real successful and that's good cause you owe me eighteen years worth of food and rent."

"Get the hell out of here," I hiss, trying desperately to de-escalate the scene rapidly unfolding.

He laughs and continues further into the brewery. "A party for the Mayor. That's pretty big, boy. Never thought you'd amount to shit, but look at you."

"I believe you were asked to leave," Callum says, crossing his arms, standing between me and my father.

"I believe I'll be having a beer while I wait for my son to get my goddamn money," he replies, clearly drunk. His eyes are still the same as they were when I was younger—angry and sullen, with a glassy sheen that speaks of too many nights spent drowning his sorrows. His face has aged over the years, deepening the creases around his mouth and making the crow's feet at the corners of his eyes more noticeable. His once robust frame has grown gaunt, his skin now sallow and sagging, with a scruffy, unkempt beard adding to his disheveled appearance. The smell of alcohol clings to him, mingling with the faint, stale odor of sweat. His clothes, wrinkled and stained, hang loosely on his thinning body, completing the picture of a man who has seen better days.

"Go wait outside for me," I say, trying to get him out before he causes an even bigger scene.

"Go back to the party. Make sure everything is still running smoothly," Callum hisses at his brothers and sister.

Anya has tears running down her cheeks and I feel like I can't breathe. I've destroyed her and now my punishment is so much worse because my father is about to destroy us all.

"Mr. Mayor, how about my fucking son over there? Won't give his father the money he owes him. What do you think about that?" My father's now yelling for the whole room to hear him.

The room grows silent as my father staggers closer to the mayor, and I can't believe this is all happening right before my eyes.

I march over toward him, grabbing my father and pushing him up against the wall. There's shouting, screaming, and I swear I hear Anya's soft cries, but it doesn't stop me. I take a swing and he falls to the ground. A pile of trash crumbled on the floor.

I get a few steps away before I fall to my knees. The weight I had on my shoulders finally taking over and crushing me.

I've lost everything in a matter of minutes. My best friend, my pride, my success, and the love of my life.

"I'm so fucking sorry," I whisper, to everyone and to no one.

Chapter 25

Anya

Griffin rushes from the room like it's on fire. Somebody was smart enough to call the authorities and Griffin's father, Mr. Cole, is being carted away in handcuffs.

This is not how I envisioned this night going. At all.

I head to the back server area, and Patrick stops me.

"Are you okay, Anya?"

I brush past him, trying my best to make it to the restroom. "Just get everything cleaned up," I tell him, making sure the guests are still being taken care of.

Patrick nods, and together with Tripp's help they head back into the room to take care of the party.

I push the bathroom doors open, and Callum follows me inside. "What are you doing?" I ask him, tears falling down my face.

Luckily for him it's late, and the bathroom has nobody in it.

He crosses his arms. "What were you thinking? Griffin?"

I roll my eyes. "First, you are not the boss of me. I can date whoever I want. And I *will* date whoever I want."

Callum leans against the counter, pushing a hand through his hair. "Do you know that this brewery is everything to me?"

I cross my arms over my chest. "Yeah, I know."

He shakes his head. "I don't think you do. I've never fought harder for something of mine ever. Like I don't know what I'd do if I lost it all." He studies me, like he has more to say, but doesn't know if he should. Then he continues, "Do you know I have nightmares all the time about losing this place?" He paces the small bathroom floor. "I don't know what I'd do. I'd feel like the biggest fucking failure."

For the first time in a long time I see my brother for the man he is. I always thought Callum had everything together. That he was so well put together, and just a grump because he thought he could be. Now I see it's not bravado that makes him this way, but lack of it.

He's scared.

Plain and simple. He's a man afraid of losing everything, and I can't fault him for that. But, he needs to know he can't put that weight all on his shoulders.

"It's okay to fail," I start off, "But you have to let us help you win. Life is all about winning and losing…" my words are cut off when he rolls his eyes.

"Please don't tell me it's how you play the game, or some bull-shit like that."

I laugh lightly. "I wasn't. However, that works here too. You can't expect this whole burden to be on you. If we fail we fail as a team, as a family. But you have to enjoy it when you succeed, and although tonight is probably one of the major failures, I think the brewery will be fine. You've made something great here. You all have, and I'm so proud. It's why I wanted to come and work here, because I wanted to be part of this magical thing that you all created."

His face grows solemn once more. "I appreciate that, but why Griffin? We're like a family here. He's like my fucking brother." Callum's voice raises a little at the end of his sentence.

"Cal, he may be like *your* brother, but he's *not* like mine. I have a lot of brothers. Some would say maybe too many," we both laugh a little, "but I don't see Griffin like a brother to me. I love him."

Callum's eyes grow wide. "Love?"

"Yes," I say, squaring my shoulders, lifting my chin. "I love him. And he loves me."

Callum shakes his head. "Anya, I'm sorry. I just felt like it was weird that Griffin was like a part of our family, that you two would see it that way too."

"Well, we don't. But who knows, maybe one day he really can be your brother."

"Oh my god, are you two already talking about marriage?"

I smile wide. "No, but you never know."

"Does he feel the same? Having his father show up here tonight makes me worry about him. He ran out of here. When we were younger he'd shut down after an altercation with his dad."

"Do you think he will again?" I ask my brother.

Callum shifts on his feet, rubbing at the back of his neck. "I don't know. Maybe you should go and find him."

"What about the party?"

Callum smiles, and for the first time it's a real, legitimate smile. One I haven't seen him have in a long time. "I've got the party. I think we can turn things around."

"Ooh, give them my chocolates. Everything's better with chocolate."

My brother offers a large, boisterous laugh. "Sure."

When we exit the bathroom, there's only one place I need to be—with Griffin.

I head to Griffin's house, knocking on the door with both fists, but there's no answer. I've tried texting him numerous times, but he hasn't responded.

Where is he?

My mind tries desperately to think of where he can be, but I can't come up with anything. Did he go to his parent's house?

Maybe to talk to his mother?

Is he down at the jail?

I'm about to leave when I hear something in the backyard. I head through the gate, worrying about what I might find.

Please don't let it be a wild animal.

"What are you doing here?" Griffin's voice greets me, but it's so dark I can't see him.

"Where are you?"

"On the roof of the shed."

I glance at the shed, making out his lone figure up top. "Can you help me up?" I ask him, wondering if the little shed can even support us both.

He helps me up, showing me where to place my foot to be able to get up here. "What are you doing here?"

"I came to check on you. Callum said when you were younger and you'd have a fight with your father you'd retract."

"Retract?"

"Yeah, distance yourself from others. I don't want you to do that with me." I scoot closer to him, and he doesn't move.

"Why would you ever want to be with a guy like me? Can't you see I come from bad genes? I think you deserve better."

He's wrong, so very wrong. I've never wanted or needed someone like this. His past doesn't define him. He's nothing like his father. He never could be. Yet, he did keep us a secret because of a promise, which hurts.

"Are you kidding?" I reach for his hand, but he pulls away from me. "Griffin?"

"I'm serious. My family's a mess. I'm a mess."

"No you're not. Look at everything you've overcome in your life. Your family does not define you. You're not him. You'll never be like your father."

His eyes meet mine, shining in the light of the moon. "Anya, I feel like I've let everyone down. You. Your brothers."

I sigh and look up at the dark sky before glancing back to him. "Why did you lie to me? When I asked you about keeping our relationship a secret, why didn't you tell me about making a promise to Callum? Did you ever intend on telling anyone or did you think we could forever keep this secret?"

He shakes his head as he stares out into his yard. "I was scared, Anya. If I told you that Callum said you were off limits, you would've went crazy. You would've confronted him and I was terrified it would end our friendship and possibly end my career at Atta Boy." I go to interrupt, but he continues. "And the idea of losing you, I felt like I couldn't breathe. I'm no better than my father, keeping secrets and hurting everyone I love. I was trying not to let anyone down and in the end, that's exactly what I did."

The pain and regret is so thick in his voice that it's hard to listen to. It did hurt when it all came out at Atta Boy, but seeing how rejected he feels breaks my heart. He's had more rejection in his life than any one person deserves. I will never hurt him by making him feel like he's any less than he is.

"You haven't let me down." I reach for his hand again and this time he takes mine in his. "You haven't let my brothers down either. I had a talk with Callum. I think he's going to be okay with it." I bump his shoulder. "I mean, he's going to have to be, right?"

Griffin smiles, squeezing my hand tighter in his. "Yeah, he's gonna have to learn to get on board with it." He grips my face with the other hand. "I'm sorry, Anya. I never meant for everything to come out like this."

"I know you didn't and Griffin," I say, waiting for his eyes to lock with mine. "You are so much better than your father. You didn't keep a secret to hurt anyone, you did it to protect everyone, to protect us."

He nods and searches my face. "Never again, I promise you that. I will never keep a secret again. If you can forgive me I promise I will give you the world."

"I forgive you, Griffin," I whisper.

He rests his forehead on mine and lets out a ragged breath. "I love you, Anya. I want to be with you always."

I smile wide, kissing him square on the lips. "And I want to be with you too."

Epilogue

Griffin

"Hey, just checking in to make sure everything is good for the party tonight," Anya says, smiling as she walks into the kitchen at Atta Boy.

I toss the towel over my shoulder and meet her, wrapping my arms around her waist. "Everything is good, baby," I say, pressing a soft kiss to her inviting lips.

"Ugh, please, I'm so happy for you guys but I don't need to see that shit," Callum says, interrupting us.

Anya and I laugh, pulling apart.

"I won't apologize for that, but again, I'm sorry about my father the other night," I say, feeling the shame wash over me once again.

Anya grabs my hand, giving it a squeeze, as Callum rests his hand on my shoulder. "Please stop apologizing for him. The scene didn't prevent Atta Boy from gaining this huge popularity. You did nothing wrong. We made sure your father was trespassed, so if he ever tries to come back he'll be arrested. The party continued with very little mention of what happened because Tripp, Brock, and I stepped in. That's what we do for family. This is your business, your reputation. Both are more important to me than anything else. So please, Griff, stop," Callum says.

After my father came and made that scene, I knew I was in the wrong by punching him, but at that moment I was already out of my mind. I was scared I'd lost Anya, Callum, and my part of Atta Boy. My father was just the icing on the metaphorical cake.

After Anya came looking for me and I knew without a doubt that we were solid, I called Callum and apologized for my father. I told him I would never apologize for falling in love with his sister and he appreciated that more than anything.

Things are now getting back to normal and by that I mean the fire that my father caused inside me is out. I have my girl, I have my friends, and I have my career.

My life, despite having a shitty start, is turning out damn good.

It is hard for me to keep my hands off Anya at work and most of the time I don't care. I told Callum I'm not hiding my feelings for her no matter who's around. He chuckled at the time, but now he continues to make a point that he doesn't want to see it. Which causes Anya and I to laugh every time.

Carol and Don were very excited about the relationship. Carol knew before anyone, but once it came out she, of course, had everyone over for Sunday dinner. Don pulled me aside and told me he couldn't have chosen anyone else he'd trust with his daughter's heart. This time I made him a promise that I will forever keep—I promised her heart will never be broken by me.

Of course I catch teasing from all the Atwood boys, but that's nothing new. It just reminds me how close we all are.

"I've told him this, but maybe hearing it from you will help," Anya says, pulling me back to the present.

I look between both of them and nod. "Thank you."

Callum grins and looks at Anya. "I wanted to talk to you, but it seems our schedules never line up."

"What's up?" she asks.

I smile, knowing exactly what he wants to say.

"I'd like to offer you a permanent position here at Atta Boy. You've proven yourself and your idea ten-fold. I'd be a fool to let you go. What do you say?"

Her eyes widen as she looks between me and Callum. A huge smile takes over her face and she lets go of my hand to hug her brother. "Yes! Oh my God, yes." She pulls back and shakes her head. "I love proving you wrong."

"Hey, you proved me wrong once. Let's not get carried away," he says, chuckling.

She wraps her arms around my waist and my arms on instinct hold her close. "Actually, I think it's twice. Griffin and I both proved you were wrong when it came to us being together."

"You're fucking right about that, baby," I say, kissing the top of her head.

"Yeah, yeah. You guys are the dream couple, blah blah blah," he says, shaking his head.

Anya and I laugh as I reach out and grab his shoulder. "Maybe it's time you let someone in."

"Maybe it's time for you both to get back to work," he says, turning and leaving the kitchen.

"I tried."

Anya turns to face me as we keep our arms around each other. "Don't worry about him. I'm sure he'll be the last of us to find someone. Paxton and I have found our forevers."

I sink my fingers into her hair and tilt her head to keep her eyes on me. "I found my forever."

I lean down and capture her lips, kissing her with all the love I feel. She moans into my mouth and I feel my dick react and as much as I don't want to, I pull away.

"Baby, you moan like that again and neither of us will get any work done today," I say, raising an eyebrow.

"Remember it for tonight," she whispers.

I lean down and nip her ear before I say, "Not something I need to be reminded of. My dick is a constant reminder."

"Making it difficult to walk away." She sighs.

I kiss her full lips and step back. "You think it's difficult to walk now, wait until we get to my place."

She groans and I chuckle. "Get back to work." I toss her a wink and smile. "I love you."

She grins as she starts to back away. "This party better be worth the wait."

"Always is which is why we're also going to celebrate you taking the permanent position. I'm so proud of you."

"Thank you," she says, her eyes bright with excitement. "I love you, Griffin."

She walks out of the kitchen and I get back to work with a smile on my face.

My heart always skips a beat when I hear those words. Anya and I are going to have a beautiful life, full of love, amazing sex, and delicious food.

━━

Want more Anya and Griffin? CLICK HERE to read a steamy bonus epilogue!

Want more of the Atwood's? You can grab Paxton and Hartford's story RIGHT NOW by CLICKING HERE!

Want to read about Harrison and February? The owners of Pour Some Sugar On Me Coffee Shop? CLICK HERE to check out their love story!

All of the Atwood's are coming soon, keep reading for MORE. Check out the first chapter of Don't Fall For Your Grumpy Neighbor, Shepherd and Felicity's story

>>>

Sneak Peek Don't Fall For Your Grumpy Neighbor

Chapter One

Felicity

This will be my first holiday without my fiancé, Karl by my side. That asshole stole three years of my life, and I've got nothing to show for it except a pile of debt and a bad case of the lonelies. Not that I'd have stayed with him to drown out the lonelies. No way. He left me at the altar, and I am *not* ok with that.

He told me he loved me. We were creating a life together. I wanted children. And I thought he did too.

I went through all the stages of a bad breakup, and sure, I cried for a few months but then my best friend, Hadley, told me I needed to get back out there.

Date.

I'm *so* not ready for that.

She, however, says I am.

Either way, I don't plan on dating anyone anytime soon. My plan is to get through this holiday season as drunk as possible. I grab a bottle of wine, and sit at my dining room table, glancing outside.

My neighborhood is a quaint little subdivision with fun and laughter. Everyone gets along, and for the most part, I love my neighbors.

Except for *him*.

Shepherd Atwood.

The neighborhood grump. While everyone else enjoys the company of others in the neighborhood, Shepherd keeps to himself. Which I wouldn't mind so much if he were indeed a good neighbor, but he's not.

Like right now.

Leaves from his yard blow into mine, piling up and creating twice the work for me to do. Why can't he rake his leaves like everyone else in the neighborhood? I should just go over there and give him a piece of my mind.

My anger boils, and I breathe in deep. Yes, I'm going to go and tell Shepherd Atwood exactly where he needs to stick his rake.

Wait. Oh my god.

My Christmas deer lighted display is gone. I look down the street, wondering where on earth they've gone. They didn't just run away.

It was a three-piece set. A father, a mother, and a little deer-ling. I even named them. Freddy, Freida, and Frou-frou.

My eyes scan my yard, and the only thing littering the lawn is the leaves from Shep's yard. All of my Christmas decor is gone.

The lights.

The reindeer.

The Santa statue at the end of my driveway.

Missing.

What the heck?

That's when I see it. A hoof sticking out of *his* trash container on the side of his house.

I leap to my feet. He threw my reindeer away.

Oh, this is *not* the day.

He can not throw away my decor on the very day I'm feeling sorry for myself. I'm going to go over there and yell at him.

I'm going to knock on his door and—Oh, I'm just so mad. I don't know what I'm going to do just yet. But it'll be something to teach him a lesson.

I stare out my window, picturing what he'll do when I yell at him. How he'll look when I'm cursing him out.

His intense eyes get lodged in my brain, and I'm momentarily stunned just thinking about him.

Did I mention he's handsome?

A very handsome jerk.

He's on his porch, and I narrow my eyes on him through my window.

He's large, a man's man, and in charge. Muscles bulge behind his flannel, and his jeans fit him snugly. I've only seen him a handful of times, but from what I've seen, I can tell he works out. Or maybe he has a job that requires him to use his hands.

I wonder what the exact shade of his eyes are. I've only talked to him once, and he was rude and cold. Bitter about my Christmas lights last year shining into his bedroom window.

Karl told me to let it go. But I couldn't stop obsessing over Shepherd and his complete lack of holiday cheer.

Fast forward to this year, and he's completely the same. I don't think the man even knows what a holiday is.

More leaves blow from his yard to mine, and it pisses me off even more. I'm going over there. Even if he's sexy. And I haven't had sex in a really long time.

Why did my mind even go there?

I shake my head, setting down my wine glass. I don't need any more liquid courage. All it's doing is turning me on as I stare down my sexy-as-sin neighbor who I can't stand.

I shrug on my jacket, and stalk outside.

I'm going to give him a piece of my mind. He stole my Christmas decor. I'm over it. I'm over the leaves. I'm over his lack of cheer. And I'm over him flaunting his sexiness for me to see every day and night.

Who needs that?

Not me.

⎓

CLICK HERE to PREORDER TODAY! Don't Fall For Your Grumpy Neighbor releases July 2nd, 2024.

The Magnolia Ridge Series

In the small-town of Magnolia Ridge there lived a family. The Atwood family had five sons and one daughter, and one day they'd all fall hopelessly, madly in love with their other true half.

Fall in love with
The Magnolia Ridge Series:

DON'T FALL FOR YOUR BEST FRIEND, Paxton and Hartford's Story

DON'T FALL FOR YOUR BROTHER'S BEST FRIEND, Anya and Griffin's Story

DON'T FALL FOR YOUR GRUMPY NEIGHBOR, Shepherd and Felicity's Story

DON'T FALL FOR YOUR FAKE BOYFRIEND, Brock and Willow's Story

DON'T FALL FOR YOUR EX-BOYFRIEND'S
BROTHER, Tripp and Millie's Story

DON'T FALL FOR YOUR GRUMPY HUSBAND, Callum
and Violet's Story

Acknowledgments

Thank you so much for reading Anya and Griffin's story. I love writing in this world, and I hope you'll continue on in the series with me.

Thank you so much to all the members of my ARC team, and all of the members of my Facebook group, The Logangsters. I appreciate all the love and support. Thank you.

About the Author

Logan Chance is a USA Today, Top 20 Amazon, KDP All-Star, and KDP All-Star UK bestselling author with a quick wit and penchant for the simple things in life: Star Wars, music, and smart girls who love to read. He was nominated best debut author for the Goodreads Choice Awards in 2016. His works can be classified as Dramedies (Drama+Comedies), featuring a ton of laughs and many swoon worthy, heartfelt moments.

Sign up for his newsletter to stay up-to-date with new releases: CLICK HERE!

Also by Logan Chance

The Magnolia Ridge Series:

DON'T FALL FOR YOUR BEST FRIEND, Paxton and Hartford's Story

DON'T FALL FOR YOUR BROTHER'S BEST FRIEND, Anya and Griffin's Story

DON'T FALL FOR YOUR GRUMPY NEIGHBOR, Shepherd and Felicity's Story

DON'T FALL FOR YOUR FAKE BOYFRIEND, Brock and Willow's Story

DON'T FALL FOR YOUR EX-BOYFRIEND'S BROTHER, Tripp and Millie's Story

DON'T FALL FOR YOUR GRUMPY HUSBAND, Callum and Violet's Story

The Gods Of Saint Pierce

SAY MY NAME

CROSS MY HEART

CLOSE YOUR EYES

ON YOUR KNEES (Benedict and Eva), Coming Soon

Magnolia Point

TEMPTING MR. SCROOGE

LATTE BE DESIRED

The Taken Series

TAKEN BY MY BEST FRIEND

MARRIED TO MY ENEMY (BOOK ONE)

MARRIED TO MY ENEMY (BOOK TWO)

STOLEN BY THE BOSS

ABDUCTED BY MY FATHER'S BEST FRIEND

CAPTURED BY THE CRIMINAL

Men Of Ruthless Corp.

SOLD TO THE HITMAN

The Trifecta Series

HOT VEGAS NIGHTS

DIRTY VEGAS NIGHTS

FILTHY VEGAS NIGHTS

Vampire Romance

Wicked Matrimony: A Vampire Romance

A Never Say Never Novel

NEVER KISS A STRANGER

The Playboy Series

PLAYBOY

HEARTBREAKER

STUCK

LOVE DOCTOR

The Me Series

DATE ME

STUDY ME

SAVE ME

BREAK ME

Sexy Standalones

THE NEWLYFEDS

HARD RIDE

THE FAVOR

RUIN'S REVENGE

HATED BY MY ROOMMATE

COLD HEARTED BACHELOR

Holiday Romance Stories

FAKING IT WITH MR. STEELE

A VERY MERRY ALPHA CHRISTMAS COLLECTION

STEP-SANTA

HOLIDAY HIDEOUT

Steamy Duet

THE BOSS DUET

Box Sets

A VERY MERRY ALPHA CHRISTMAS COLLECTION

ME: THE COMPLETE SERIES

FAKE IT BABY ONE MORE TIME

THE TRIFECTA SERIES: COMPLETE BOX SET

THE PLAYBOY COMPLETE COLLECTION

FILTHY ROMANCE COLLECTION

THE TAKEN SERIES BOX SET: BOOKS 1-3

Made in the USA
Middletown, DE
05 July 2024

56859827R00137